Hunter Holt might be the most stubborn ex-soldier ever born, but when he's called on to help find a lost foster kid, he jumps into action. Even if it means working with the woman who broke his heart five years ago—the woman who still haunts his dreams . . .

Faye Smith has spent five long years trying to get her life back on track. She knows she should've turned toward Hunter and not away from him. But they both had too many demons to destroy. Maybe now they'll get another chance—and save someone else's life too . . .

But first they'll have to stop arguing long enough to trust the Deep Ops team. Hunter was a lost boy himself once. In fact, he ran away from the exact same man, their monster of a father. Now he and Faye will have to unite to find the brother he never knew—and maybe each other . . .

Books by Rebecca Zanetti

The Dark Protector series
Fated
Claimed
Tempted
Hunted
Consumed
Provoked
Twisted
Shadowed
Tamed
Marked
Talen
Vampire's Faith
Demon's Mercy
Alpha's Promise

The Realm Enforcers series
Wicked Ride
Wicked Edge
Wicked Burn
Wicked Kiss
Wicked Bite

The Scorpius Syndrome series
Mercury Striking
Shadow Falling
Justice Ascending

The Deep Ops series
Hidden
Taken novella
Fallen

Published by Kensington Publishing Corp.

Taken

Deep Ops

Rebecca Zanetti

ZEBRA BOOKS
Kensington Publishing Corp.
www.kensingtonbooks.com

Chapter One

To say that things hadn't ended well for them would've been the understatement of a century—heck, of the entire existence of human beings on Earth. Even a caveman breakup, with swinging mammoth bones and the throwing of fire, would've seemed like an afternoon at the beach compared to the day Faye and Hunter called it quits.

Which explained why her hands were sweaty and her tennis shoes kept tripping over the exposed tree roots of the barely-there path on the way to his cabin. Pine trees closed in from every direction, and an animal squawked in the distance. The sound probably came from a bird, but the beast sounded like it had teeth. Did some birds have teeth? She'd had to toss a decapitated bunny off her deck last year because of a sociopathic owl hunting the forest behind her house. So if not teeth, then maybe claws.

At the moment, she'd rather face that owl than Hunter Holt. He would not be happy to see her, and he'd be downright hostile to the news she was bringing. Dread and anticipation boiled inside her at the prospect of seeing him again. Her first love. Heck, her only love. Man, he'd been everything.

Maybe he'd gotten fat and bald in the past five years and had taken up smoking, which would give him wrinkles. The thought cheered her. Then hopefully she'd stop having dreams about him that resulted in her seeking a cold shower.

She turned a corner, and the side of his cabin came into view. It faced the Smoky Mountains and Dogwood Creek, which rushed by surprisingly fast for late June. A tumble of large rocks angled up from the water to a man-made stone wall designed to protect the wood and rock cabin from flooding.

He came out from the rear of the cabin, his gait easy, his gaze alert. No doubt his bizarre instincts had warned him of her approach half a mile down the trail. "Faye."

Ah, shoot. Neither fat nor bald. In fact, the bastard looked better than ever. "Hunter," she said, drawing on years of practice to keep her voice level and calm.

His intense blue eyes, the color of a male indigo bunting in the height of mating season, revealed absolutely no emotion. His dark blond hair was cut short and yet was still shaggy—thick enough for a woman to spend some serious time running her hands through it. Despite the short beard and mustache he wore, the hard angles of his face proved he'd grown even more handsome in the past five years. His chest had broadened, and cut muscles shifted beneath the worn cotton of his shirt. "What are you doing here?"

Had his voice deepened? She held her stance on the trail, the toe of her shoe angled on a rock. "Miss Angelina sent me."

Finally, emotion. His eyebrows rose, and he moved toward her as if unable to help himself. "Is she okay?" Urgency roughened the edges of his southern accent.

"She's fine," Faye murmured, something hurting inside her chest. Would he have had the same reaction if somebody had approached him about her? After all these years, the good and bad, would he have cared one bit if something happened to her? Not that it mattered. Not anymore. "She wants our help. That means…" Faye lifted a shoulder.

He sighed and tucked his thumbs in his front pockets. "We help."

She nodded. The man might be one of the deadliest on the planet, and the crankiest, but when Miss Angelina called, you went, no matter who you were, or who you'd become.

"Why send you?" he asked.

Ouch. Seriously. Double ouch. "I'm the only one she's been able to reach so far," Faye said, her hand all but itching to grab a rock and hurl it at his stubborn head. The stone facade of his face was starting to piss her off, and he probably knew it. "Would it kill you to have a cell phone?"

His frown deepened. "I have a cell phone, and Miss Angelina has the number. Called me just last week."

Huh. What in the world did that mean? Faye tilted her head. "And she hasn't called you yesterday or today?"

"Nope."

Well. That was interesting, and not just a little disconcerting. Everything in Faye wanted to hand off the case to Hunter and head back to figuring out what do with her life in Louisville. But Miss A had been insistent that Faye work it to the end, and there was some logic there, considering Faye had once been a shrink. A mistake among many in her life. She drew off her beige backpack, because her shoulders were starting to ache. "Perhaps Miss A wanted me to deliver these to you."

His gaze dropped to the pack, and then he sighed. "You might as well come inside, then."

"How could a girl refuse such a gallant offer?" she snapped, holding the pack with her good arm and starting for the green-painted side door.

The quickest flash of a smile lifted his lips for a moment. When she came abreast of him, he reached for the backpack.

She jerked it away. "I've got it."

"It looks heavy." He reached for it again, his long arm easily snaking across her body to grasp the strap.

"No." She pulled again, engaging in a tug of war reminiscent of when they were kids. Finally, she twisted her torso, and he either had to let go or pull her entire body toward him.

He didn't let go.

Instead, he grabbed both straps and pulled, jerking her up against his much harder and taller form. His scent of man and wild maple hit her so fast she gasped as memories flooded in. "When are you gonna learn that life isn't fair?" He lifted, and she had no choice but to relinquish the bag or somehow grow ten inches. "You're five-four, a buck twenty, and in a physical fight, you're not gonna win."

"Five-five," she retorted, releasing the bag and instantly punching him in the gut as hard as she could. Pain ripped from her wrist up her arm. His darn ribs were steel.

He sucked in air, pained. "I'd forgotten your sucker punch."

"You're a moron." She turned away, pissed beyond belief that she'd lost the backpack.

"So you've said, on more than one occasion," he drawled, back in control again. "In fact, I believe that's the last thing you yelled at me."

"Actually," she said, looking over her shoulder directly at him, "I believe it was 'I love you, and I'm sorry.'" Then she turned and shoved open the door to his cabin.

* * * *

The words hit him in the chest so hard he couldn't move. Those *had* been the words. And she'd been sad, not angry, accepting and not willing to fight any longer. They'd hung around him, inside him, for so long they'd become a part of him.

What the holy fuck was Faye doing at his cabin? The one place in his life she'd never touched, and now she was there. He'd have to burn the place down once this situation was over—after he had a few choice words with Miss Angelina for creating this disaster.

He sighed. He'd never have choice words with Miss A. She'd probably whack him with a wooden spoon, the way she had when he'd been a hurt, angry teenager.

Maybe that's why he and Faye never had a chance. They'd started mad and wounded, and that's how they'd gotten to know each other. Even now, more than a decade later, they'd just had a tug of war over a stupid backpack. Then she'd punched him in the stomach. It didn't matter that he'd been the one to teach her to hit without injuring her wrist or fingers. The memories all hurt.

Shaking himself out of it, he followed her into the lower level of his cabin, which held a TV room, kitchen, guest bedroom, and bath. The upstairs was a massive master bedroom and bath he'd designed and built himself on top of the existing structure.

She pulled out a chair at the round wooden table, facing the wide windows with a view of the creek. "Might as well get started."

He swallowed. There were so many words to say, he couldn't find one. Damn, she looked good. Straight blond hair cut in a sassy style, soft brown eyes, girl-next-door good looks. Her skin was still smooth and freckled, and her eyes lively, even with the tired lines showing stress.

The stress concerned him. Had she not healed in the last five years like he had? If he had? Shit, sometimes in the middle of the night, when nightmares woke him, he wasn't sure he had. "How are you these days? Faye Rockefeller?"

She rolled her eyes. "No. I've stuck with Smith so far. I'll change it once I find the right one." She'd hated her father, so she'd been trying on new last names as long as he'd known her.

"What's going on, Faye?" He dropped the pack in the center of the table.

She opened the top and drew out several brightly colored manila file folders.

He sat, his gaze on them. "Miss Angelina's folders." The woman loved folders. His youth—the good times, anyway—had been punctuated with colorful file folders. For school planning, for chores, for different seasons. Seeing them was like being yanked back to happier days. "What are those?"

Faye flipped open a purple folder to show a picture of an angry looking blond kid of about seventeen, with minor scruff as a mustache. "Meet sixteen-year-old Jackson. One of Miss A's newest kids. She only had him for one day. He's run away."

Hunter tugged the picture closer with the pad of his index finger. "Kids run away from foster homes all the time—even Miss Angelina's." He'd been one of those kids who ran away. Twice. Miss A had found him and brought him back the first time, and he'd fought his way back, tail between his legs, the second time. But she hadn't gloated. Nope. She'd taken one look at him, her pretty brown eyes somber, and told him to go wash his hands for dinner. It had been that easy. He didn't leave again until he joined the Marines.

Should've stayed home. Maybe then he and Faye would've had a chance. He kept his gaze on the photograph. "Think if we'd started that band like we planned we'd have ended up like this?" He didn't talk to anybody, but he'd never been able to keep his mouth shut around Faye. Apparently that hadn't changed.

"I don't know," she whispered. "I've thought about it. If just one of us had taken a different path, or even if we'd all faced a crisis at a different time, would we have been able to help each other? Maybe if Mark hadn't died…"

Hunter looked up, noting the delicate bone structure beneath her pale skin. Who'd been protecting her the last five years? Oh, she had a mean temper, and he'd taught her to fight, but Faye had always had a fragility that scared the shit out of him. Of course, he'd seen her wounded and broken as a kid, her arm busted up, too many bruises across her pretty face to count. That image would never completely fade.

She rubbed her chest. "I left flowers on his grave before I drove down here."

Guilt filtered through Hunter. When was the last time he'd visited Mark's grave? The man had died a hero, fighting for his country far away from home, and Hunter couldn't even bother to visit. But sometimes he figured Mark was around, watching over them. He wasn't in that grave. Not really. Bones didn't count in this life. He cleared his throat and looked back at the picture of the kid. "What's his story?"

She swallowed. "Took off with a thirty-five-year-old teacher, thinking she's the one. She's knocked over two restaurants, as well as a gas station, and so far none of the video shows he's an accomplice."

If the kid was with her on the crime spree, he could be charged regardless. "He in love?"

"Thinks he is," Faye muttered. "The teacher's name is Louise Stockley, and she left behind a husband, another teacher. I'm doing research into her history. We think the affair started last year, when she was his math teacher."

Disgust ripped through Hunter. The woman had preyed on a lost kid in foster care—one no doubt with some anger issues if his picture was to be read correctly—and taken advantage of him. "Aren't the authorities on this?"

Faye nodded, her hands nervously tapping the other file folders. "Yes, but Miss Angelina is really worried and wants us to put our skills to use. You're the best tracker ever born, and you were trained by the military to be even better." The last was said with a perfect imitation of Miss A's accent. "And that's not all." Her voice wavered this time.

Awareness pricked its way up Hunter's spine. "What?" he asked.

Her hand shaking imperceptibly, Faye reached out and slid the picture to the side, revealing a foster care intake form. "His full name is Jackson Holt. Look at him. I mean, *really* look at him. He's the spitting image of you at sixteen."

Chapter Two

Faye wanted to suck the words back in the second she said them, but Hunter had to know the truth. He showed no reaction, not even a twitch of an eyebrow or a shift of his shoulders. Instead, he just studied the picture. For minutes. Then, his hand shockingly steady, he picked up the intake form and started to read.

Faye shivered. The river rushed outside, and birds chirped merrily in the trees. Yet the silence inside the cabin, hot and suffocating, threatened to choke her.

Finally, he set the form down. "So the S.O.B. was alive as of six months ago."

"Yes," Faye said, having already read the forms, flashing back to the game they'd played as kids. When it was storming outside, the four of them—she, Hunter, Raider, and Mark—would hide beneath one of the bunkbeds at Miss Angelina's and think of the worst ways their fathers could've died. They were all bad men, and her favorite fantasy had been that they would kill each other. As far as she knew, the monsters had never crossed paths. "Are you okay?" she asked.

Hunter scrubbed both hands down his face. "Yeah. It's not surprising. I mean, Ramsay was good with the ladies. Who the hell knows how many half-siblings I have out there?" He looked back at the picture. "Sixteen years younger than me. Hell. I could be this kid's dad."

"Except I never got pregnant," she whispered. They'd been faithful to each other—she knew that in her bones.

"The kid would've at least had a chance if he was ours and not my dickhead of a father's," Hunter said, pushing the picture back onto the stack, glancing at the intake form again. "Instead, the mom dies when he's four, and he ends up with Ramsay or whoever Ramsay left him with for the last decade or so." He rubbed at a scar across his collarbone. "I wonder if the asshole still throws knives when he's angry."

Faye's damaged arm hurt, as if in response. Her father had broken it three times before the authorities sent her to live with Miss Angelina. The smell of whiskey still made her want to puke. She shoved away the bad memories. "I wanted to wait until I told you before calling Raider in." With Mark dead, it was only the three of them now.

"Raider's busy with a new assignment, and it seems like his head is on right," Hunter said.

She couldn't explain it, but the three of them needed to do this together. "Miss Angelina wants him in on this," she said.

"Well. I guess that's that, then." Hunter drew a cell phone from his back pocket and pressed speed dial, putting the phone on speaker in the center of the table.

"Hello, brother," Raider answered, a barking dog in the background.

Hunter drew back. "Did *you* get a dog?"

"Shit, no. He's kind of the team mascot, and he's the craziest son of a bitch you've ever met," Raider said. Something shuffled. "Shut up, Roscoe," he bellowed.

The dog barked louder.

Hunter's lips twitched. "What is he barking at?"

"A damn cat. Well, kitten," Raider said, his bootsteps heavy through the phone. He slammed a door, and quiet descended. "I'm in an interrogation room just so I can talk. There is no discipline here." The last was said as a low growl.

God, it was good to hear his voice. They talked at least once a week, but she needed to hear him right now as she faced Hunter. Faye let the sound warm her. "Hey, Raider. How are you?"

Silence. Complete, stunned, heavy silence. Then he cleared his throat. "Is Miss Angelina all right?"

Hunter rolled his eyes. "Yes, she's fine. I know it's a surprise to hear that Faye and I have stopped throwing punches long enough to call you."

Raider was quiet in that way he had. "Is one of you dying?"

Faye sat back in her chair, amusement zinging through her. "No."

"Am I dying?" Raider asked.

Hunter tapped his fingers on the table. "No. Geez, you've gotten dramatic."

"Holy shit, you two are back together. I knew it. I always said if one of you pulled your head out of your ass, it'd work out. It's nice to be right. I mean, I usually am." His low voice rose in animation and what could only be termed happiness.

Faye jerked, her stomach cramping. "No. We definitely are not back together." Regardless of the fantasies she'd had through the years.

Hunter keep his blue gaze on the phone and didn't look up at her.

Raider sighed, the sound amplified through the speaker. "So you're both still morons. Good to know." A tone of pure frustration came from him next. "All right. Nobody is dying and you two are still idiots. The anniversary of Mark's death isn't until next month, and I'm sure we're not planning a summer camping trip like we used to. What is going on?"

Faye bit her lip. Should she let Hunter explain?

"My bastard of a father had a kid who was relocated to Miss Angelina's. He's run away," Hunter said.

Well. That was a quick explanation.

"Okay," Raider said, his voice cautious. "That's a lot."

Hunter's chest hitched, and dark amusement crossed his rugged cheekbones. "I know you're busy with the new gig—"

"If you need me, I'm there," Raider said.

Hunter sucked in air in a rare show of emotion. They were all there for each other—no matter what. Faye's hand itched to take Hunter's like she would've so many years ago, so she set it on her lap. She no longer had the right to touch him.

Hunter shook his head. "You can run point from there for now. I don't want to screw up what you have going on."

Faye cocked her head. "What exactly do you have going on?" He had better not be thinking of going undercover again. Last time had nearly killed him, and knowing Raider, this new unit was completely ignorant about it. In fact, she'd bet her bottom dollar that he was still working the case that had gotten him hurt. "Raider?"

"I'm just a handler in this new unit," Raider said. "Don't worry."

Hunter looked up at Faye, his gaze narrowing. She nodded. Their best friend was a horrible liar. He was still working that case.

"Well," Faye said, going in for the kill. "Miss Angelina asked that you work on this with us."

Hunter gave her a look, and she shrugged.

Raider sighed. "Then I'll be working that case with you. Please send me everything you have so I can prepare on the way. I'll wrap things up here tomorrow and be at the cabin on Friday, and I'll expect you to be there too, Faye. See you then." He clicked off.

Triumph filled Faye. So there. She'd get a visual on Raider herself. She smiled.

Until the back door opened, and a naturally stunning blonde poked her head inside. "Hunter? I thought we were meeting down at the fishing hole." She came all the way inside, all five-foot-eight of her, and smiled. Her jeans were tight and her denim shirt a perfect match for her intelligent green eyes. "Oh, hi. Sorry. I didn't know you had company." She set her hand on Hunter's shoulder.

* * * *

Hunter nearly smacked his head. "Dana. Shit. I'm sorry." The fishing hole was a slippery hike, and nobody should do it alone. "I got caught up." He gestured toward Faye. "This is Faye. Faye, this is Dana." His gaze caught on Faye, and she looked even more pale. Worse yet, her eyes had gone that deeper brown that showed she was about to either bolt or punch.

Dana released his shoulder and leaned over to shake. "Hey. It's nice to meet you."

Faye shook hands, the fakest smile imaginable on her face. "You, too."

It hit him then. Right between the eyes. Faye was jealous? How was that possible? They hadn't been together in five years. Even so, his default impulse had been to not cause her pain from day one. "Uh, Dana is a journalist doing a piece on the guides of the Cumberland River."

Dana snorted. "Puff piece, because my editor is forcing me to take a vacation." Her emerald eyes sparkled. "They can't make me vacation completely." She strode into the kitchen and took a glass from the cupboard, heading for the fridge. "You still have that lemonade? It was quite a hike."

Faye's chin lifted, and her nostrils flared the tiniest amount.

Humor attacked Hunter for no good reason. Not one. He hid the smile because he didn't want to get kicked beneath the table. How could he better explain Dana to Faye? He shouldn't have to—not really. Yet if some guy was with Faye, he'd want to knock the asshole's teeth out. "Listen, I—"

Dana took the lemonade out. "Anybody else want some?"

"No thanks," Faye ground out.

Hunter coughed to keep from laughing out loud. "No. I'm good."

Dana poured a glass and took a drink. Red bloomed across her angled cheeks. "You put more sugar in it," she gasped, coughing. "Seriously, Hunter." Giving him a look, she dumped the liquid in the kitchen sink. "What is wrong with you southern boys?"

He lifted a shoulder. Miss Angelina had probably ruined them all with her sweet tea.

Dana finally caught the whiff of tension in the room. She faltered. "Oh no. Am I interrupting something?" She gingerly put the glass in the sink.

"No," Faye said, starting to gather the papers into the file folder. "Not at all. I was just leaving."

"No, you weren't," Hunter countered, flattening his hand over the purple folder. "We're going to come up with a plan, and it's going to take a while, so you're staying here." There wasn't a place for her to stay in town, which was thirty minutes away. "Then we'll get to work tomorrow so we have something to share with Raider when he arrives on Friday."

Faye tried to tug the file folder away, but he held fast.

Dana's sandy-blond eyebrows rose. "This is different," she mused, watching them.

Yeah. They turned into scrapping kids the second they were together. Maybe that had been part of their problem. Growling, Hunter yanked the file free and held it against his chest.

"You are such a dick," Faye muttered. She kept her gaze averted and pushed away from the table.

"Faye? You ain't going anywhere." He lapsed right back into southern around the woman.

Her small shoulders went back and she stood. "If you think I'm staying here with you and blondie, the extremely hot girlfriend journalist, you have completely lost your mind."

Dana snorted. "I've been called a lot of things, but that's a good one." She smiled and leaned back against the counter, clearly enjoying herself.

"You are not helping," Hunter snapped, giving her a look.

She shrugged. "Not really trying to help."

Faye faced Dana. "Listen. I'm sorry for swearing and for making this uncomfortable. I'm sure you're a lovely person."

"I really am." Dana grinned. "Everyone says so."

What a smartass. "Dana," Hunter said, also standing, his temper awakening, "is my boss's daughter and a very good friend. She's also off a bad breakup with a dumbass she never should've been dating, and I believe she's sworn off men." He hated explaining himself, and he really disliked talking this much. Damn Faye. "Even if she hadn't sworn off men, we are just friends, and that's all it can be, because she's a keeper, and I stay far away from those."

Faye crossed her arms, looking even angrier than she had before. "And why is that?"

His temper blew. "Because I'm the type of guy who only loves once, and you walked away."

Chapter Three

After a sleepless night in Hunter's guest room, Faye sat in the passenger side of his truck, her temples aching. All night his words had run through her head. She had walked away, but they'd both given up. Hurt, angry, and lost…neither one of them had been in a place to help the other through Mark's death, not to mention the disasters their lives had become. Now, with distance, she saw the situation clearly. "Did you get help with the PTSD?" she asked, trying to admire the gorgeous red maples out the window.

"Yes," he said shortly.

"I wish I could've helped you," she murmured, wondering if the slight give in the seat was the years-old impression of her butt. Why hadn't he ever gotten a new truck? She'd lost her virginity in this one, and it was disconcerting to be sitting in it so many years later. Disconcerting and intriguing.

"I wish I could've helped *you*," he countered, his voice level and unemotional. "I knew you were struggling after quitting being a shrink."

Yeah. She'd missed signs, and a patient had committed suicide. The desperation in him had eluded her, and she'd made a mistake in trying to be a psychologist in the first place. She'd been trying to understand her own childhood, she now realized. She should've just sought counseling and found another dream to pursue. Something that kept her outdoors and happy. But Mark had died right when she was picking up the pieces of her life, and the world had disintegrated again. "You were right. I shouldn't have been a shrink."

Hunter made a low sound, one she couldn't decipher. "You can be anything you want. I just thought you were seeking answers in a way that wasn't good for you."

And he'd been right. As usual. In order to survive his childhood, Hunter had developed instincts about people, about life in general, that most people couldn't imagine. Even so, his own emotions blinded him. "Mark's death wasn't your fault." He said he'd dealt with it, but she still needed to say the words. "You were a continent away when he took that bullet." She turned back to see his strong hands clench the steering wheel.

"He wouldn't have joined up if I hadn't," Hunter said, his voice hoarse.

That was true. There was no way to make that fact not true. Mark had idolized Hunter from the first time the police dropped him off at Miss Angelina's. "He was a good soldier, and he saved a lot of lives." Maybe if Raider had been available and not undercover when the news came in, things would've been different. Raider didn't even discover the truth until three months after Mark's body was brought home. Talk about screwing a guy up for a while. "Mark would be pissed if he knew you carried guilt around because of him."

Hunter snorted. "That's true. Man, he had a temper."

Didn't they all? Even though the past hurt, the release in finally talking about it healed something inside her. "Are you enjoying being a guide on the rivers?"

"I am." He turned onto the interstate, heading for Kentucky, and the truck rolled like it was brand new instead of decades old. "The quiet of the water is soothing, and we get some pretty fun groups out for a day or two. Corporate groups. The challenge is to keep them from drowning." He grinned.

Her shoulders relaxed into the well-cared-for leather. "I always thought you'd go back into law enforcement. With your tracking skills."

"I've been approached," he acknowledged, speeding up to pass a semi.

The rest of the trip was made in silence until they pulled up in front of the police department in Shelterville, Kentucky. For a moment, they sat outside the whitewashed brick building, gathering their thoughts. Neither had particularly good memories of the place.

"You know the new chief?" Hunter asked.

"No," Faye said, her stomach jumping all over. Then she spotted Miss Angelina walking down the sidewalk dressed in a nice pink suit. Joy grabbed her, and she reached for the door handle.

"Wait a minute." Hunter grasped her arm and leaned to look around her. "She's wearing a hat."

Faye stiffened. Miss Angelina was wearing a wide-brimmed, fancy pink hat with a flowered band. The woman only wore hats when she went to church or war. "What does that mean?" Shrugging off his hand, she opened the passenger's side door and jumped to the ground, reaching Miss A in long strides for a rose-scented hug. "I have all your files safe in my pack like I promised. Nothing has been wrinkled." This feeling had to be what coming home was like.

Miss Angelina hugged back, surprisingly strong for a seventy-year-old woman. Then she leaned back to take a good look at Faye, her brown eyes clear. "Are you all right? I was worried sending you out to that cabin in the middle of nowhere by yourself."

"I found it easy enough." Faye smiled and moved out of the way so Hunter could lean down—way down—and hug the person who'd pretty much saved their lives. Faye took a moment to study the woman she loved more than she could love any biological mother. Miss Angelina's salt-and-pepper hair came to her shoulders in springy coils that Faye had loved to play with as a kid. Her brown skin was still smooth, with generous laugh lines at her eyes and lips. She was a woman who laughed often and well, spreading her joy to kids who needed it. But put a wooden spoon in her hand, and homework got done. Fast.

"Hunter." Miss A patted his stomach. "You're not eating enough." She shook her head, her wide hoop earrings swinging. "If you're going to guide on the river all day, you need protein. A lot of it."

"Yes, ma'am," Hunter said. "I'll do better."

Shoot, Faye wished she had that effect on the man. Maybe she should invest in a wooden spoon.

"Let's go, then." Miss Angelina hooked her arm through Hunter's, and he straightened even taller, escorting her around the sidewalk to the front door. Then he opened the door for them both.

Miss A swept inside first, nodded at the deputy behind the counter, and continued beyond that down the long hallway to the chief's office. The sergeant, a fifty-something bald man named Huey, just nodded and let her go on her way. Nobody messed with Miss A.

They reached the office in the back, and she knocked on the speckled glass window in the door.

"Come in," came a low voice a with strong southern accent.

They walked in, and Faye got her first look at the new chief. About forty, black hair, blue eyes, slight paunch beneath his uniform. His face was smooth shaven and a mite round. He sighed. "I told you I'll call with any updates."

Hunter instantly moved past Faye and Miss A, taking the lead. "Is that how you greet your constituents?" His southern drawl came out full force as well, and he looked around, his frown showing he didn't approve of the office in the slightest.

Faye swallowed and stepped closer to Miss A, who could probably level them all with a simple sentence. Even so, she didn't like the chief's demeanor any more than did Hunter.

The chief sighed. "I apologize. Hello, Miss Angelina." He turned narrowed eyes on Hunter. "Who are you?"

Faye winced. Not a good start. She moved forward before Hunter could say anything that would get them kicked out. "I'm Faye Smith, and this is Hunter Holt. We're here to help."

The chief's eyebrows rose. "Holt? As in Jackson Holt?"

"Apparently," Hunter said. "Guess he's my half-brother. It's news to me."

Miss Angelina cleared her throat. "This is Chief Mullins. He was appointed by the mayor last year."

Ah. Mayor Mullins must be a relative. Faye nodded. "It's nice to meet you." She partially turned to see a cork board on the side wall with Jackson Holt and Louise Stockley's photographs tacked to it, the word "Suspect" above them.

Hunter followed her gaze. "The kid is a victim. Not a suspect."

Mullins hitched up his belt. "I've been talkin' to folks who know that kid, and he's a bad seed. No doubt he'll be charged as an adult in these crimes—if he survives the manhunt."

Faye's breath caught. "It's our understanding he hasn't been present at any of the robberies."

Mullins shrugged. "They're on a spree together." He rocked back slightly on his heels, his hand settled comfortably on the butt of the gun at his waist. "Louise Stockley was out on bond for statutory rape because her husband found out about her and the kid. Then she went on the run. Not only are law enforcement personnel after them, but so is a cadre of bounty hunters who are gonna shoot first and ask questions later. You might want to prepare yourself for how these things usually end. Considering you're kin and all."

Hunter's chin lowered.

Uh oh. Heat flushed down Faye's esophagus.

Hunter studied the chief. "Just how many of these sprees have you investigated, chief?" he asked with a sardonic edge.

Mullins's eyes flashed. "That, like this case, is none of your business."

"As kin, I have a right to know," Hunter retorted, looking like one long line of danger.

"You don't have a right here," Mullins drawled. "You didn't even know the kid existed."

Miss Angelina drew herself up. "I do have a right, since I'm Jackson's foster guardian. So please do your job and fill me in on the status of the case."

The chief sucked in air, filling his chest. Finally, losing the staring contest, he pointed to a map beneath the pictures. "The lady has hit gas stations from here to the state line, and it looks like she just hit one in Indiana, heading northeast. We have a Kentucky manhunt in full force, and we're reaching out to friends in Indiana right now. Those two won't get away, and if they won't give up, it's gonna get bloody."

"That kid gets hurt, and you answer to me," Hunter said, his hand closing into a fist.

Mullins faced him and only paled slightly. "I've heard about you. Big tough marine who washed out and came home to fish. Why don't you return to the river and let the professionals do their jobs?"

Hunter smiled, and the sight was nowhere near pretty. "Chief? I have absolutely no doubt you couldn't find your ass with both hands."

Miss Angelina pressed her lips together, her eyes sparkling. She cleared her throat. "Chief Mullins, I'm aware that you and Louise Stockley were, ah, friends. This must be difficult for you."

The chief's nostrils flared.

Faye jerked. Friends? What kind of friends? She kept silent for now.

"That has nothin' to do with this," Mullins spat. "Now I'd like for the three of you to leave. Interfere with this case, and I'll have you arrested, no matter your high standing in this town." The last was obviously directed toward Miss Angelina.

Hunter opened the door. "Your threats are a bad idea, buddy."

Mullins partially smiled, making his eyes look even beadier. "You're not in a position to speak with me, Holt. Your whole family is a waste. In fact, I just talked to your daddy down at Sunny's Tavern this morning. Guy doesn't have much good to say about you or your brother."

Tension shot through the room, heating the oxygen. Hunter's expression closed down.

Crap. His father was in town? Faye reached for his arm, needing to touch him. This was a disaster. "Let's go, Hunter."

Triumph filled Mullins's face. "It has been a pleasure."

Hunter took Faye's hand, his grip firm. "I can see this office is being poorly run. It's a pity. For now, this isn't your case any longer, chief." He nodded, and Miss Angelina swept out, followed by Faye, who kept his hand and waited to make sure Hunter didn't lunge at the jackass.

"The hell it ain't," Mullins sputtered.

Hunter glanced at the map. "If they've crossed lines, this just became a federal matter. And oddly enough, this washed-out marine still has plenty of friends in high places." He smiled, and his eyes glittered in a way that made Faye shiver. "Y'all have a nice day now," he said, shutting the door behind them.

Chapter Four

Rage was an ugly feeling. Hot and desperate and out of control. The two women in Hunter's life who'd taught him to deal with it were right beside him, walking into the nice spring day, both with concerned looks on their pretty faces. Faces he'd loved for years. "I apologize for my language in there."

Miss Angelina pointed a fob to unlock her spunky light green Volkswagen bug. "That's all right. You'd certainly make a much better chief than him. That man is definitely a horse's patoot."

Faye snorted, and Hunter couldn't help but smile. It took a lot for Miss Angelina to use such language, and it had always been a delight to her kids. *Her kids.* How many had she saved through the years? At least fifty. "I'll get the new information to Raider, Miss A. Since this is a federal case now, we'll see if he can get his people involved. He says they're the best."

"Of course they are." Miss Angelina turned and patted Hunter's chest, her gaze somber. "Deep ops has always been a specialty for each of you." She sighed and glanced down the street before focusing on him again. She tilted her head. "I'm not going to ask you to refrain from doing what you're about to do."

"Thank you," Hunter said. He'd never defied her, and he couldn't start now, but he needed to do this.

"Just don't get arrested," she said, slipping into the driver's seat of her car. "That chief would love an excuse." She angled her neck to look at Faye. "Keep him out of jail."

"Yes, ma'am," Faye said, her hand still in his. She had light calluses on her palm—no doubt from gardening, which she'd always loved to do. Even so, her skin remained unbelievably soft and her bones small.

Miss A nodded. "I have to get to the store. We're expecting a new shipment of honey vanilla syrup for the lattes." She shut the door, ignited the engine, and zoomed away from the curb. Two bicyclists dodged out of her way, followed by a couple of other cars.

Faye sighed. "She didn't hit anything this time."

It was an improvement. Hunter looked down the quiet sidewalk in the direction of Sunny's Tavern. The crappy old place was several blocks away, across the railroad track and beyond several closed businesses and deserted buildings. Everything in him tightened to impenetrable rock.

"Let's do this, then," Faye said, taking a step forward.

He held her in place. "I need you to stay in the truck, or walk down to Miss A's store." How many hours had they spent working at the specialty ice cream and latte store? More than he'd ever been able to count. "Please."

"No." Faye tightened her fingers through his. "Why would I do that?"

He looked down at her, needing her cooperation. "Because if you go with me, Ramsay will insult you, and I'll put my fist through his face." There was so much truth in the statement that he paused to let it sink in with her. "I need to talk to him and try to figure out where Jackson is going, if he has an idea. We have to get to that kid before somebody shoots him." Mullins wasn't the only trigger-happy jackass out there, and now bounty hunters were on the move.

Faye faltered.

He released her hand. "On the way to Miss A's, call Raider and fill him in, would you? We need to get him officially on this case as soon as possible." Then he gave her a slight nudge. "You need to trust me, Faye Smith Oliviet Jude Phillips Carter Ford June Berry."

She smiled, as he'd wanted her to. Her hatred for her father had extended to her last name, so she'd changed it every month or so while they were growing up. "Fine," she said, turning. "But I'm giving you thirty minutes with him. That's it." Her cute butt swayed in her worn jeans as she walked down the sunny sidewalk.

Thirty minutes was all he'd need. Any more time than that, and he wouldn't be able to control his temper. He strolled down the sidewalk, past the respectable businesses, to the rougher buildings with bars on the windows, to boarded up warehouses. The grass went from green to burned brown to just plain old dirt. His gut ached, and his temples pounded. Finally, he reached Sunny's.

The name had to be ironic. Even back in the day, the name would not have fit. Pine needles covered the worn metal roof, while the wooden siding had warped from weather; its dingy, rust-colored paint worn white in several places. The sign above the door was missing one of the n's.

Nausea swirled in his stomach, and his palms sweat in a way they hadn't for a decade.

He pushed the thin door open, and the stench of stale smoke made him want to turn away. Instead, he stepped inside the dim interior, banishing all emotion. A jukebox in the corner played a song about dogs and war, while several down-and-out patrons were scattered along the bar or at low tables. The reddish carpet was hard and bristly from years of spilled alcohol and puke, while the walls were velvet that had once been red.

He spotted Ramsay instantly.

His father sat to the far right, at a table against the wall, his back to it. He partially leaned over a full glass of whiskey next to a bottle. No ice. Ice was for pussies, he had always said. He straightened, and somehow his shoulders had broadened in the last decade and a half. His eyes, as blue as Hunter's, gleamed.

Hunter ignored the kick to the gut and forced himself to walk casually toward the table, as if he had all the time in the world.

Did the bastard know he could kill him with one decent move? It wouldn't be the first time he'd killed. Not even close. "Ramsay." Hunter pulled out a scarred wooden chair, flipped it around, and straddled it. There couldn't be anything between him and the door—not even a seat back.

"Hunter, boy." Ramsay leaned back and looked him over. This close, his belly showed some fat, as did the skin beneath his chin. He had to be, what? Fifty by now. Just that, though. "How long has it been?"

"Well, now. I had the stitches taken out eighteen years ago," Hunter drawled, rubbing the scar along his collarbone.

Ramsay smiled, revealing tobacco-stained teeth, and the scruff along his jaw showed more salt than pepper. "You always were a stubborn shit. That knife barely nicked you."

"You always had shitty aim," Hunter returned. But decent reach. He'd taken a punch from the bastard more than a few times.

"How's your aim?" Ramsay asked.

According to Hunter's military record, absolutely superb. "Almost as good as my shot." Which was also the truth. He was one of the best snipers still alive today, and part of that job was hunting and outsmarting the next guy. Which he needed to do right now, no matter how badly his hands itched to strangle the breath out of the man who'd fathered him. He angled his head, looking at Ramsay's long hair. Blond and gray—thick to the shoulders. "At least you kept the hair." That boded well for him.

Ramsay cackled. "I knew you'd be a tough one."

"You don't know me at all," Hunter said.

"Sure I do. Heard you washed out of the marines and spend your time playing in the river with corporate assholes." Ramsay took a healthy drink of his whiskey.

Hunter forced a smile. Small towns held no secrets. "Actually, I was honorably discharged, with a boatload of medals you've probably never heard of. Unlike you."

Ramsay's eyes narrowed. "I was railroaded."

"Bullshit. You were caught stealing and dishonorably discharged." Unfortunately, that meant the dickhead had returned home and knocked up Hunter's mother. Or so-called mother. "Enough reminiscing. Tell me about the kid."

Ramsay took another drink, looking like a fat cat eyeing a bird. "What kid?"

Hunter flattened his hand on the table. "Ramsay? We should get a couple of things straight here." His chest heated and his accent deepened, but he was fine with that.

"What's that, boy?" Ramsay took another deep drink, finishing the glass this time.

"I killed a lot of people in the service." Hunter lowered his chin and met a blue gaze way too similar to his. "Every single time, whether it was through a scope, with a knife, or even with my hands, you know what I imagined?"

"That it was me." Ramsay smacked his too-red lips together before they curved into a pleased smile.

Hunter let his eyebrows rise. "Um, no. I imagined I was making the world safer for somebody." He allowed himself to smile. "I haven't thought about dirtbag scum like you for eons. The second I took the stitches out with a rusty screwdriver, you ceased to exist." Miss Angelina had showed up real fast, with a wooden spoon and some alcohol spray to make sure he didn't get an infection, however. "Did you really think I'd remember you?" Hunter drawled.

"Well. You're here." Ramsay poured more rotgut into his glass.

"I'm here about the kid. Where would he go?"

Ramsay set the bottle down, his hand shaking. "The kid is on a joyride, banging some cougar. Let him live a little."

"Like you did? I saw pictures of the bruises across his ribs." Hunter ground his back teeth together. The kid had only been twelve, according to the dates on the pictures, and somehow he'd ended up back with Ramsay for more abuse. "Where would he go? Where have the two of you been?"

Ramsay sighed. "I guess I could remember."

Anger flushed through Hunter so quickly he nearly swayed. "I ain't givin' you money. Now talk, or I swear to God I'll show you exactly what those of us *not* kicked out of the marines learned to do with morons."

Ramsay rolled his eyes, but his hand shook as he took another drink. "Fine. I don't know. The kid mentioned something about the teacher having a cabin on some lake in Washington. My guess is that the cougar is driving the bus."

"Jackson's mom was way too young for you."

"There's no such thing, my boy." Ramsay's eyes glittered. "She was a sweet little gal who died way too young. Loved that kid. A lot." He smiled. "Unlike your mama. That bitch took one look at you, decided she didn't want two of us, and took off faster than a raccoon chasing a garbage truck."

"So you've said," Hunter murmured, not giving a shit. She probably wasn't even alive. "Anything else you know about the kid?"

"Just that his temper is worse than yours. And that's sayin' something." Ramsay took another drink, and some of the liquid spilled onto his protruding belly, soaking his shirt. "Has an odd fondness for root beer floats from that old restaurant—Tommy Toms? Probably somethin' that reminds him of his mama. She liked it there, too."

It wasn't much, but it was a start. "Just how many kids are out there with your curse?" Hunter asked.

Ramsay tried to wipe off the wet spot on his shirt. "Hell if I know. There could be more, but you and Jackson are the only ones I've had to deal with."

If there were others, they were lucky not to realize their heritage. "Fair enough." Hunter pushed back from the chair, ready to get out of there.

Ramsay looked up. "What about you? Any chance I'm a grandpa?"

Bile rose in Hunter's throat. "You'll never be a grandpa." He turned and strode out of the place, sucking in several deep breaths as clouds began to gather outside. Even if he had twenty kids, he'd never let one of them near the bastard. His collarbone ached and he rubbed it, turning back toward town.

A release wound through him. A surge of acceptance with a heat of freedom. He'd faced his past, and Ramsay was just a fattening drunk who couldn't touch him. Never again. He'd won. Finally.

Now he had to help Jackson.

He quickly dialed Dana, who answered on the first ring. "Hey. I need you to dig into a story for me, if you don't mind. Just reach out to some of your contacts." He gave her the lowdown on Jackson and the teacher, and then clicked off. Maybe they could figure out how to find the kid.

He needed to see Faye.

Chapter Five

Faye settled on the wooden rocking chair, moving slightly, a cup of tea in her hands. The creek rushed along in front of her, and she watched the water go by. Hunter had been silent on the way back to his cabin, and after a dinner of grilled cheese sandwiches, he'd disappeared upstairs to get some work done. Apparently there was an office next to the master bedroom.

Charm and beauty spread out before her, and she mentally planned where Hunter should plant bushes and more stone rocks when he had the chance.

Darkness had fallen, while the moon glowed big and luminous. Maybe full. It was hard to tell when it was so bright. The trees melded together on the other side of the water, looking dark and mysterious.

The deck creaked, and Hunter stepped outside, settling his bulk into the adjacent rocking chair. He put his bare feet up on the wooden railing. The frayed edges of his worn jeans covered his ankles. "I'd offer you wine, but I don't have any." He rocked quietly.

"I'm fine with tea." She'd never been one to drink.

He nodded. "Yeah. Me too." His feet looked big and strong and somehow sexy. "I drank bourbon after Mark died, for the first time ever, and it was a disaster. Figured being out of control was a bad thing, so I haven't had a drop of the hard stuff since. Beer is enough for me."

That made sense, too. "We've both seen the bad that alcohol can do." Or maybe their fathers were already bad, and the alcohol had just helped them to cope with it. Anyway, who cared? "I still throw up at the smell of whiskey."

Hunter rolled his neck. "Miss A keeps me in the loop, and she said you're thinking of going back to school."

Faye lifted a shoulder. "Maybe."

"To do what?" he asked.

She flattened her hands on her jeans. "I'm not sure yet." Then she pointed over to a set of trees. "You should plant tulips there for next spring." She grinned. "Though you'd have to pee on them every night to keep the deer away."

He chuckled. "What else?"

She straightened. "Well. What about a bench surrounded by flowers over there?" She gestured nearer the water.

He stared into the darkened night. "Why don't you study gardening? Or landscape design?"

Heat filled her face. "I've been thinking about it." How did he always read her mind?

"You'd be great at it, Faye." He rubbed his hands down his jeans and laid his head back, closing his eyes. "Ramsay pushed my buttons."

"Figures." She set her tennis shoes on the railing, relieving the tension in her lower back. "I gave it fifty–fifty odds you'd hit him."

"Thought about it." Crickets competed with the sound of water over rocks. "But then I figured he'd win. If I become like him, even for a second, he wins."

God, she missed this. These quiet moments with Hunter Holt and nature around them. "He'll never win, Hunter."

"You still have nightmares?" he asked, his voice low in the night.

"Yes. Mainly when I get stressed." Horrible ones, where she was a kid again, hiding from her monster of a father. She wished she could remember her mother, but she'd died young. "But not about the patient who committed suicide. I've handled that. It's the ones from childhood that never go away. You?"

"Mine get mixed up." He sighed, the sound heavy and a little lost. "Sometimes they're of Ramsay when I was young, and sometimes I see the faces of people I shot through a scope. Every once in a while, it's Mark asking why."

"Yeah," she whispered, her heart aching at the thought of the cute redhead who'd been a younger brother to all of them. "Miss Angelina has his flag on her fireplace mantel in a very pretty case."

"Raider carved that case," Hunter said. "One of his many hidden talents."

Something was missing. Faye plucked at a string on her jeans. Hunter was saying all the right words, but a distance remained inside him—between the two of them, but definitely inside him. Was he still angry? It felt like it. "How often do you have the nightmares?" she asked.

He shrugged. "Who cares?"

She did. Always had, and always would. He wasn't the only one who'd given his heart away and never gotten it back. That left them exactly nowhere, especially if he still wasn't dealing with everything. "Hunter—"

"I'm not yours to worry about anymore, Faye."

The words cut hard and fast. Ah. This was why they'd broken up. Or at least it was one of the reasons. He'd had five years, but apparently it wasn't long enough. "You'll always be mine," she surprised herself by saying. "You, Raider, and me. We'll always have each other." Even if they couldn't be together, they were family. Whether he liked it or not.

His feet dropped to the wooden planks. "On that note, I'm gonna—" He stiffened and turned toward the path through the forest. Then, smooth and silent, he stood. "Go inside, Faye. Now." He drew a gun from the back of his waistband.

A gun? While just sitting on the porch? "What's happening?" she whispered, jumping to her feet. The wooden chair rocked back and forth from her suddenness.

He angled his body to the edge of the porch, his gun pointed down, the sinewed muscle of his forearms tensed.

She moved behind him, looking into the darkness. Nothing seemed out of place.

He lifted his head. "Two men. Coming this way." He glanced over his shoulder. "I told you to go inside. Do it and turn off all the lights. Now."

She backed away toward the sliding glass door.

"Hunter? Don't shoot me, brother," Raider called from the darkness.

Faye halted. Her chest expanded, and her arms tingled. "Raider!" She ran full bore toward the end of the deck.

Hunter clotheslined her around the waist, drawing her up short and forcing the air from her lungs. "Get behind me," he hissed.

She coughed, her eyes watering. "What the heck?"

"He's not alone."

"So what?" She winced as he set her down and her lungs filled. "What is wrong with you?"

Raider emerged from the trees on the path. He wore a black leather jacket, dark jeans, and a button-down shirt. Moonlight glinted off his short black hair. "You couldn't extend your driveway to the cabin? It's quite a hike."

"Who's with you?" Hunter asked.

Another man walked out—this one beyond huge. He stood about six-six with a broad chest in what had to be a specially made leather coat, one battered and well worn.

"This is Clarence Wolfe," Raider said, striding toward them over the rocks. "He's with my unit."

"Hi," Clarence said. "Call me Wolfe, or I like to hit people."

Wolfe it was. No problem. With a happy cry, Faye launched herself from the deck. Raider caught her easily, lifting her off the ground and hugging her hard. "How's my girl?"

"Great." She kissed his chin and held him tight. While she and Hunter had gone a different direction before crashing and burning, Raider would always be her brother. She leaned back to look at him. "I swear, you get better looking every year." It was true. Raider was part Japanese, and his blazing black eyes had always fascinated her.

"So do you, sweetheart." He set her gently to the side. "Faye Dunnaway? McGillicudy? Jordan? Who are you this week?"

She rolled her eyes and gave her standard explanation. "Still Faye Smith. I haven't found the right last name yet."

Raider grinned. "Faye, this is Wolfe."

The giant held out a hand that swallowed hers past the wrist. "Hello. I'm here to back Raider up in case anybody tries to hurt him."

She grinned. "You look like good backup."

"I truly am." Wolfe had buzz-cut brown hair and light brown eyes. Several healed knife wounds showed along his forearm. "You're pretty. Are you dating anybody?"

Raider tugged her hand free from Wolfe's. "You can't date my sister."

Wolfe looked from one to the other. "She can't be your sister."

Faye's hackles rose. "Oh yeah? Why not?"

Wolfe's eyebrows lifted into his hairline. "You sound southern, with a very cool accent. Raider does not. Families should sound the same."

Her mouth gaped open and she angled slightly away. "Is he serious?"

Raider sighed. "Yes, and he's genuine." He let his southern accent, the one he'd fought so hard to banish, out with the words. "Is this better?"

Wolfe drew back. "Dude. You're southern?"

Raider nodded. "Yep. When I started learning languages with Homeland Defense, I worked on diction. The accent is too easy to identify."

Wolfe grinned, looking like a lethal puppy. "That's cool. I like your real voice." He frowned. "Hey. Why can't I date your sister?"

"Because one of my brothers already did," Raider muttered, looking up at Hunter. "Put the gun away."

A meow caught Faye's attention, and she turned again just as a cute little furry white head poked out of Wolfe's pocket. "You have a kitten in your pocket." The kitten had bright blue eyes and one mangled ear. It twitched the healthy one.

"Yeah. That's Kat. K.A.T. He's part of our team," Wolfe affirmed.

Faye tried to keep her mouth closed as she looked up at Raider, who nodded. What in the world? Raider was paired with a formidable-looking guy who kept a kitten in his pocket? Was her brother finally loosening up a little? "This is interesting," she murmured.

"Isn't it, though," Hunter drawled from the porch, slipping his gun back into place. Now, there was a southern accent. It licked right down Faye's spine to pool in her abdomen. She barely covered a shiver.

"Ah," Wolfe said, his gaze narrowing on her. "Now I get it."

* * * *

Hunter kept his gaze on the soldier with the kitten in his pocket even as Raider approached. While the guy seemed harmless—aside from his size—he'd already scoped out the entire area, river to forest, without moving his body an inch. His hands were loose, but one rested near an obvious bulge beneath his jacket. He moved like he'd been well trained, and if Hunter didn't miss his guess, he'd been on a team. Maybe not a SEAL, but definitely some sort of special ops team. He just had that look.

Raider reached him, climbed two stairs, and they hugged.

Something loosened inside Hunter's chest. Something that had been tightening inside him since Faye had shown up at his place. "I've missed you, brother," he said.

Raider released him, his dark gaze serious. "I've missed you, too. Now that I have a steady gig outside of DC, and now that you're here for good, we're gonna be better about seeing each other."

Hunter nodded, his gaze sliding back to the threat. "Is your buddy nuts?"

Raider ducked his head to the side. "Jury is out on that one." He turned and watched Wolfe try to charm Faye while unobtrusively angling his body between her and the forest—the only direction from which a threat could come. "But he's solid, and he has my back, which means he has yours, too."

That was good enough for Hunter. And it was nice to meet some of the folks in Raider's life now. "Wolfe? Why don't you come on in? We have some leftover sandwiches if you're hungry."

Wolfe waited until Faye had walked in front of him before nodding. "I could always eat."

Yeah. The guy had to weigh about two-sixty, and all of it looked like muscle.

"I don't have any cat food," Hunter said.

Wolfe shrugged. "That's what my other pocket is for."

Of course it was. Hunter waited until Faye reached him, and then he gently pulled her in front of him toward the door. This Wolfe guy was a few cans short of a six-pack.

The moment everyone had entered the living room, a sense of claustrophobia threatened to take control of his lungs. He lived in the middle of nowhere for a reason, and it had been a long time since he'd had so many people in his haven.

Faye eyed him for about two seconds and then announced she was going out to the porch.

Sometimes he hated how well she knew him. It had been five years since they'd touched, and she instantly was trying to help him, even though she'd been the one to leave. Oh, he understood why. Didn't make it any easier to live with. "I'm fine," he said, taking a deep breath.

Raider stepped toward the kitchen, unslung the pack around his shoulders, and set out a stack of paper. "We can go outside if you want."

"No." Hunter would have to deal with people at some point. Might as well be the people he cared about. "What do you have there?"

Raider spread the papers out while Wolfe made himself at home and started rooting through the refrigerator. The kitten's head was up and swinging from side to side as he looked inside as well. Wolfe brought out a tomato, and the kitten swatted at it.

Hunter angled closer to the table when he recognized a picture of Jackson Holt. His half-brother. "What have you found out?"

"I checked all witness reports as well as surveillance cameras, and so far, the kid hasn't committed a crime. Well, he's not on tape, anyway." Raider smoothed a hand over his clean-shaven jaw. "Two witnesses, at least, confirm there wasn't a kid when Louise perpetrated the crimes."

Hunter tucked his thumbs in his jean pockets. "If we can get to him in time, we might have a chance." He looked over his shoulder, where Faye was leaning against the doorjamb of the open sliding glass door. "What are your thoughts? I know you haven't been a shrink in a long time, but…"

She sighed. "Jackson's pathology is easy. He grew up without a mother, with an abusive father, and his teacher fulfills a maternal need he probably doesn't know he has."

Wolfe turned around. "She's sleeping with him."

Faye nodded. "Yeah. I'm sure it's confusing as heck. He's sixteen and attracted to her, and she's fulfilling several needs. I have no doubt he'd kill for her if asked." She pursed her lips. "Although it's telling that he hasn't been at any of the crime scenes."

"How so?" Hunter asked.

Faye looked down at the scattered papers. "Either she's protecting him, which is likely, or she doesn't trust him."

"Protecting him?" Hunter growled. "The woman is a pedophile. She's committing statutory rape."

"And she's wrong, and should be convicted," Faye said gently. "But she must have issues, or she wouldn't be doing this. We've asked for background information on her, but I haven't seen anything yet—mainly because the chief of police won't share. Usually in this situation, a female teacher who sleeps with an underage male student is unfulfilled at home, or abused, or just looking to be the center of attention."

"Does it matter?" Wolfe asked, leaning against the refrigerator and rocking it back against the wall.

"Not really," Faye acknowledged. "But if we understood her better, we might get at least an idea of what she'll do next. Of what we can do to protect Jackson. The more we know about her, the better off we are."

Raider nodded. "Yeah. We've had pushback from the local chief of police, and I've called in my boss to deal with him tomorrow."

Hunter paused. So they were going to meet more of Raider's team. That was good.

Wolfe grinned. "You'll like Angus Force. He has a dog."

Raider lifted an eyebrow. "That reminds me: hide the booze."

Was Force an alcoholic? Hunter didn't like the idea of Raider trusting a guy who had to have booze hidden from him. They needed to discuss this.

Wolfe looked around and then winked at Faye. "So. Where am I sleeping tonight?"

Chapter Six

Hunter didn't sleep much, even now, so when the back porch creaked just after dawn, he sat up in bed. The footsteps were sure and heavy—Wolfe. Apparently Clarence Wolfe didn't sleep any better than Hunter did. Thunder roared up above, and rain splattered hard against the roof and windows, assisted by a pissed-off wind. It drowned out all other sounds, and soon even Wolfe's footsteps faded into the storm.

Maybe the soldier was going running. As long as he didn't try to make another move with Faye, Hunter didn't give a shit. When the guy had given her the kitten to sleep with, she'd lit up like one of those flashlight apps. Wolfe had been charming, but also seemed not to take anything seriously, including himself. What was his story, anyway? Hunter needed to sit Raider down for a chat sooner rather than later. Maybe this new HDD unit wasn't such a great idea for his brother right now.

While Mother Nature kicked ass outside, the interior of the cabin remained quiet and still. Faye was in the guest room, Raider on the sofa, while Wolfe had grabbed the recliner—for some of the night, anyway.

A scream had Hunter out of bed and running for the back porch, his gun already in his hand. He nearly collided with Raider, and they quickly shifted into sync, scouting the cabin and heading toward the door to the deck.

Faye emerged from her bedroom, her hair mussy, the kitten wide-eyed in her hands. "What?"

"Stay inside." Hunter slipped into the rain, his gun down.

An angry female voice caught his attention first. "What in the holy hell are you doing? Who are you?" Dana came into view, being hauled across the rocks by a determined-looking Wolfe.

"Ah, shit," Hunter muttered, his shoulders relaxing. "Let her go, Wolfe."

Raider lowered his SIG Sauer slowly, his gaze ultra-alert. "I take it you know her?"

This was nuts. "Yeah." Hunter opened the door so Wolfe could drag a struggling Dana inside. She elbowed him in the gut, and his jaw tightened, but he didn't let go.

Hunter followed them inside. "She's a friend, Wolfe. Let her go."

Dana shoved Wolfe, her blond hair matted against her face and her pink raincoat soaked. She kicked him in the knee once for good measure as he released her arm.

"Hey." Wolfe leaned down and rubbed his knee. "Was that necessary? You're kinda mean."

Dana's eyes were wide and her face pale, making her freckles stand out. "You're crazy. This is assault and battery. What in the world?"

Wolfe shrugged, his gaze sweeping her. "You were trespassing, and it's wet out there. Figured we could discuss matters inside."

She looked like she wanted to kick him again. "That was my favorite umbrella you threw into the river."

Wolfe rubbed rain off his forehead. "Sorry. An umbrella is a weapon. Your mouth seemed sharp enough."

Hunter winced, shaking rain from his hair.

Faye came all the way out of the bedroom, still holding Kat. She wore loose leggings with a tank top that nicely outlined her breasts, her eyelids heavy and her eyes tired. "Hey, Dana."

"Hi, Faye," Dana said, angling into position to kick Wolfe again. "Cute kitten."

"He's mine," Wolfe said, easily stepping out of range. "You're pretty. You dating anybody?"

Raider scrubbed a hand through his wet dark hair and set his gun on the end table. "Jesus, Wolfe. She's not going to date you after you ruined her umbrella and kidnapped her."

Dana leaned back and took a good look at Wolfe. He wore ripped jeans, unbuttoned, and his chest was broad and bare. There were knife and bullet wounds…and perhaps electrical burns? "You are kind of cute," she murmured.

Raider shook his head. "Unbelievable." He was bare chested, and his four-point Celtic knot tattoo swirled over his left shoulder and bicep, identical to the ones on Hunter's arm and Faye's lower back. Mark had worn his on his right bicep. Tonight, Raider wore streamlined blue sweats, and his bare chest showed some new scars: a couple of knife wounds, as well as what looked like a bullet hole near his left ribcage.

Hunter had known about the different fights, but he hadn't realized the full damage. They'd let their little family go separate ways for too long. Was it because Mark had died? Or was it because he and Faye had taken a chance on something more and blown it? Hunter fought the urge to tell Faye to go put on more clothing. "Dana? You're welcome any time, as you know, but what the hell are you doing here at dawn?"

The blonde rolled her eyes and unbuttoned her raincoat.

"There we go," Wolfe said, approval in his dark gaze.

Now Hunter wanted to kick him. "Knock it off."

Dana shrugged out of her coat and revealed a manila file folder she'd had tucked against her side, protected from the rain. "I've been called back to DC on the first flight, and I wanted to get you this information before you left. I called, but your phone went to voice mail."

Damn it. He'd probably let the battery run dry again. He hated having a phone.

Faye moved closer to him, and he fought the urge to wrap an arm around her shoulders like he would've done years ago. The kitten meowed and snuggled into her chest with a snuffled sigh. He was actually jealous of a cat.

Dana handed over the folder, and he opened it, reminding himself to concentrate on the case at hand. "Louise has taught at a couple of schools, and there were unsubstantiated concerns at the last one about a relationship with a student," Dana said. "All of the information is there, including a couple of domestic violence reports on her husband."

Faye nodded, leaning to read around Hunter. "That fits the possible pathology. Abused woman, unhappy at home, feels like a god with a kid who worships her."

"That's no excuse," Hunter snapped.

"No, it isn't," Faye agreed. "There is no excuse for what she's doing. But if we understand her a little better, maybe we can find her."

Good point.

Dana wiped rain off her cheeks. "Also, I have a contact I can't name who found a phone number that might be your brother's. The number is in here." She gave Wolfe a look and then slid a folded piece of paper to Hunter. "Of course, you'll have to charge your phone first."

* * * *

It was too early to hit another store, considering they'd fled Illinois just last night. But Louise had been determined. Jackson Holt sat on the motel room bed in Iowa, wondering why anybody had ever thought that avocado green and bright yellow went together. Even a million years ago, the colors had to have looked bad. The door opened, and Louise came in, her gorgeous brown hair swirling. "Louise." He jumped up, took the shotgun out of her hands, and threw it on the bed. Then he kissed her.

Like always, she tasted of sunshine and strawberries.

She kissed him back, holding him tight. Finally, she leaned away and drew a pack off her shoulders. "I got us some real money this time, my man." Reaching in the pack, she pulled out a bunch of bills and threw them high in the air.

He laughed, because she wanted him to. But this robbing and taking risks wasn't gonna get them anywhere. He loved her, which meant he trusted her, but this was a bad path, and he couldn't protect her when she went out robbing people by herself. Being criminals was no way to build a future, and he wanted one with her. It was their destiny. "Let's get somewhere safe, and I'll take care of you," he said, wanting to be tough for her. "It's my job to protect you." He'd be a much better man than his father had even thought of being. He sure as hell would never hit one of his kids. Or Louise.

His phone, the one he'd forgotten he had, buzzed from the plastic grocery bag holding his socks and underwear. His chest hitched for just a second at the thought that his father was calling and actually gave a shit. He hung his head, his lungs deflating. Why the hell did he care? His old man had never cared except to hit and kick. Jackson rubbed the scar beneath his right eye from the cigarette his good old dad had flicked at him.

"Hey." Louise cupped his jaw. "Where did you go?"

He smiled, leaning in to her touch. "Nowhere. Only here and now matter." It was their motto, and he needed to remind himself of it once in a while. But it was time he stepped up as the man in this relationship in a way his father never had. The bastard never could. "The next robbery—I do. Not you."

She smiled, happy lines extending from the corners of her eyes. "That's my job, baby. You know it."

His chest puffed out. "Not anymore." He couldn't let her down the way his father had hurt and then abandoned his mother before she died. "If you love me and if you want me to be your man, you have to let me."

She smiled, love in her eyes. Nobody had ever cared about him until her. He didn't understand why she liked him, but since she did, he wasn't going to screw it up. "We'll see," she said, looking at the pack.

He held her hand. "Nobody got hurt this time either, right?" They couldn't be harming people, and the more times they robbed, the more likely it became that somebody would get hurt. He couldn't live with that. "Right?"

She nodded and patted his face. "I gave you my promise that I wouldn't hurt anybody, and I haven't. The gun isn't even loaded, sweetheart. For now, I saw an older Chevy about a block over—I'll go get it. You pack up and be ready to go when I honk." She hummed happily and moved through the doorway again, shutting the metal door gently.

He turned to get ready. They had to split town fast. Again. His phone buzzed a second time, and he turned, yanking it from his pack. Then he blinked. It was a video call. His stupid dad didn't know how to do that. Louise had turned off the GPS, but he knew they should leave the phone here anyway. He swiped the screen, already talking. "Just leave us alone," he muttered as the screen focused.

A face came up. One that looked a hell of a lot like his. The guy was old, though. At least thirty. "Hi," he said.

Jackson dropped to sit on the bed. "Who are you?"

"Hunter Holt. Your half-brother," the guy said. His blue eyes were the exact same shade as their dad's. "Didn't know you existed, or I would've been in contact sooner."

Huh. A brother. Jackson's chest heated, and his ears burned. "They're pulling out all the stops now?" Man, even the FBI had to be after them now. They were like Bonnie and Clyde—or some other famous couple from history. "What rock did they roll your drunk ass out from under?" The asshole was probably a drunken, wife-beating jackass, just like their dad.

"U.S. Marines. Now I'm a river guide, mainly on the Cumberland River," Hunter said. "And I rarely drink. If I do, it's a beer, and that's it." He rubbed his short beard. "I do have a problem with mint chocolate chip ice cream, however. It's a vice."

Jackson lifted his chin. Marine? He had a brother who'd been a marine? His mind fuzzed. "What do you want, Hunter?"

"To help you," Hunter said bluntly. "I'm at the convenience store your teacher hit in Iowa, and there's a lot of blood on the floor. Smells like rust and dirt. Kinda metallic. You ever smell a bucket of blood?"

"Stop lying to me." Jackson's stomach lurched. "For the record, I've tasted plenty of it."

Hunter's eyes darkened. "I bet you have. I was raised by the asshole, too. Until I went to Miss Angelina's."

Jackson lifted a shoulder. He'd only been at Angelina's for a day, but she seemed pretty nice. Although she probably would've wanted him gone in a week like most places had in his life. "She didn't tell me I had a brother." Not that he'd given her much of a chance. He'd left the first night to get to Louise.

Hunter nodded. "I'm sure she wanted to make sure I had my head on straight first. Had some problems after leaving the service. I've found fishing and guiding on the river helps. I'd love for you to join me. Maybe get *your* head on straight. You haven't done anything yet that would prevent that."

Jackson snorted, something perking up inside of him that needed to be squished. His path was set. Louise honked outside. "Thanks, but we ain't the Brady Bunch." He'd seen the old show late one night. People didn't really live like that. "See ya, Hunter." He clicked off and threw the phone against the wall so it shattered.

Then he grabbed his stuff, the money, and ran outside to meet the only person who would ever love him.

Chapter Seven

Faye stretched out of the SUV with her backpack over one arm outside a worn-down roadside motel. They had just finished surveying the second crime scene in Iowa—this one with no injuries or death. Just a lot of ruined food and broken jars. Rain splattered down, and she lifted her face to feel the coolness. Her limbs ached and her eyes were gritty. Darkness had descended a couple of hours ago.

Louise and Jackson were long gone from this town, and Raider's friends at the FBI were trying to track them via traffic and store cameras, but the duo had become pretty good at taking back roads.

Hunter kept dialing Jackson's phone, walking out of the dingy motel office and across the muddy parking lot toward them. He'd been trying to call Jackson all day after their one phone call. Without success. Faye chewed on her lip as Hunter's shoulders went down.

"Damn it." He turned and threw his phone across the parking lot. Raider, sitting on the hood of the SUV, snagged it out of the air before it could hit a gas tank.

"Impressive," Wolfe mused, looking at Raider.

Faye barely kept from smiling. Hunter was way too frugal to destroy his phone in a temper. He'd known Raider would catch it. No reason to tell Wolfe that, however. The wind blew across the nearly vacant lot, smashing rain against her sweater.

Raider read the face of his phone. "No sign of them yet. Force was delayed in DC but will meet up with us as soon as possible. Let's sleep and be on the road early tomorrow. Hopefully we'll know where to go." Lines fanned out from his dark eyes, and his voice had gone southern rough. He jumped off the hood.

Hunter held up two old-fashioned keys with plastic yellow holders. "Two rooms only."

Faye's heart kicked up a beat—a hundred beats, actually. Was Hunter making a move? After all this time? There was only one other vehicle in the lot—a rusting and dented Ford pickup from the early eighties. "They only have two rooms available?" The place had at least fifteen rooms.

He nodded, his eyes weary. "Yes. Apparently there was a busted pipe, a mold issue, and a problem with asbestos." He didn't sound like he really cared. "The guy has two rooms available. Take them or leave them."

Oh. So no move. Her body ached.

Wolfe partially turned. "Kat usually likes to sleep with Raider. Other than that, you and me, Faye? I'll take Kat's place with you?"

Man, he was cute—in a hot serial killer type of way. She pressed her lips together to keep from laughing. At least somebody wanted to sleep with her.

"No," Hunter said, tossing him one of the keys. "She's with me."

Wolfe grinned. "Thought so."

Faye's face heated while her abdomen flip-flopped. In a motel room with Hunter Holt once again. Man, the things they used to do for fun. She tried to concentrate and not act like a total dork. "Kat the kitten sleeps with Raider?" She'd enjoyed snuggling with the kitten the night before, but he had been restless several times during the night.

"Yes," Wolfe said at the same time Raider vehemently shook his head.

"I can't wait to meet more of your team," she murmured.

Wolfe turned toward a faded pink metal door with a black sticker of the number two plastered in the middle. "We're the normal ones."

Raider rolled his eyes and followed his buddy, splashing mud up on the way.

Hunter turned and headed for door number one, letting Faye make up her mind about whether to follow or not. Not that there was much chance she'd sleep out in the car. She hesitated for only a second and then followed him into a surprisingly clean room. One queen-sized bed took up most of the space. It faced a plastic table that held an old box-style television set. The carpet was blue shag with angled vacuum marks, and a quick peek into the bathroom showed freshly scrubbed ancient tiles and a bright yellow sink.

Hunter dropped his pack on the floor. "You can have the bathroom first."

She nodded and went inside to change into a T-shirt and shorts before washing her face and brushing her teeth. The guy was acting as if they'd never slept together. Or maybe he was just worried about this new brother of his. Knowing Hunter, he was somehow feeling responsible. Her body tingled all over. It had been so long since she'd touched him, and he looked harder than ever. Would he make a move?

Would she?

Her body was all in. Her heart, on the other hand, had already shattered once when they'd ended a relationship. Did she want to set herself up for that again? Even for a night or two of probably excellent sex? There was no probably about it. Hunter had always been intense in the bedroom, and after his experiences, he'd undoubtedly be even more so now.

She shivered. Then she walked out of the bathroom, her head high, ready to face him.

He lay sprawled on the bed, his breathing easy, his eyes closed. The gun was on the night table next to him, and the door was double locked. He was asleep?

The amusement coursing through her competed with disappointment. They hadn't been together for five years, but this was the perfect opportunity to find out if they still worked. She'd missed him so much that even now, when something interesting happened, he was the first person she thought to call. But she hadn't. What if she had? What if she'd reached out once she'd gotten her head on straight? She wished she had.

Would they be having a totally different kind of night?

It didn't matter. They weren't. She shut off the light, carefully pulled back the covers, and slipped into the chilly sheets, rolling as close to him as she could. Even though he lay on top of the covers, heat still poured from him, and she shut her eyes, sighing at the familiarity, as well as everything new. She opened her eyes again to look at his strong profile.

There was no way she could sleep.

* * * *

Faye woke beneath the covers with a muscled arm banded around her waist, heated thighs pressed into the back of hers, and her shoulders bracketed by a very strong male chest. When had Hunter climbed into bed with her? Heck. When had he taken off his clothes? Desire flushed through her, tingling along her skin, through her torso, and landed with hot need between her legs. That quickly and that completely. She shifted against him, trying to ease herself into comfort, and she brushed against his rock hard erection. She stilled.

"Don't worry about it." His breath stirred her hair, his voice low and hoarse. "It's you and me. That's inevitable."

Was anything else inevitable? She closed her eyes as sensation after sensation rippled through her. "Hunter." God, she'd missed him. The feel of him all around her—the warmth of safety. They'd already hashed out what had gone wrong, so what was left to talk about? Was there any way to go forward? She'd dated in the last five years, and not one single man had come close to Hunter Holt. For the rest of her life, she would compare every man she met to him.

"What thoughts are going through your head, Faye Houdini?" he rumbled, his mouth close enough to her ear that she couldn't help but shiver.

She'd forgotten she'd used that name for almost a month their sophomore year. "You and me. Where we went wrong," she whispered. The rain continued to fall outside, fogging up the old windows, which were visible between the cheap blinds. "I told you what was hurting me at the time. What I was struggling with. About when my patient killed himself." And in typical male fashion, he'd tried to fix her instead of fixing himself. "You never told me about what happened to you over there."

"It was war," he murmured. "I was a sniper, not just because I could shoot, but because I could track. I hunted humans, and it took time to deal with that." He caressed her arm with his warm palm, and nothing had felt so good in way too long. "I can't let any of that touch you. Never could and never will. But I have dealt with it the best I can." His hand encircled her wrist, pressing in lightly. So much gentleness wrapped in raw strength. "I've always felt guilty about not protecting you when Mark died. Not being there for you."

He'd tried. She remembered. But he had been going through so much guilt and pain that he had shut down. "I wanted to help you, too. And you wouldn't let me." That had hurt more than anything else.

"I'm sorry," he murmured.

"Me too." She snuggled closer, and he groaned when her butt skimmed his erection again. Her breath heated, burning down to her lungs in harsh tingles. This was such a bad idea.

With one tug, he pulled her onto her back and rolled on top of her. "Wanna have sex?"

A chuckle burst out of her before she recognized the reason behind it. He always did get right to the point. Every cell in her body wanted to have sex. Her brain was so much smarter than her body.

He leaned up on his elbows to study her in the darkness, his groin against hers, his heated thighs between hers. "For old times' sake?"

There was no such thing. She ran her hands through his short, thick hair. "I've never made it with a guy with a beard." It was cut very short, almost more thick scruff than beard, but he looked outdoorsy and tough.

He leaned down, his mouth covering hers. Soft and sweet— seeking answers. Maybe asking questions.

She sighed at the contact, feeling like she had come home.

Then he kissed her. His lips firm and coaxing, he explored her, his tongue sweeping inside to taste. She closed her eyes and slid her hands down to his shoulders, pulling him closer, her body responding instantly to his. His muscles vibrated beneath her palms as he held himself back. As he went slowly and gently, so as not to scare her. Even after all this time, she knew him. Even as teens, he'd tried to stay sweet and gentle, wrapping himself in a control she'd always disliked. As they'd grown older, he'd let himself go a little. But after he'd returned from his last tour, he'd been different. More intense and distant. The control he exhibited now had an edge to it.

She liked the edge but not the absolute control. Kissing him back, she lifted her thighs on either side of his, allowing him more room to settle against her panties.

He growled, the sound rumbling up from his chest and into her mouth. She took that and the rest of him, scraping her hands down his flanks. He'd developed cut muscles along his ribcage and lower back. She was gentle exploring the healed scars, her heart hurting with each new raised bump or indent. He'd been through so much.

He softened the kiss, the hand twisting in her hair quickly smoothed out. She'd liked the bite of pain, but he seemed determined to treat her like glass. As if she still wasn't strong enough for him.

"I don't want gentle," she said, meaning every word.

"Too bad." His lips moved against hers as he talked, sending tremors down her body.

Oh, he didn't get to hold back. If she was taking this chance— and it was a colossal chance with her heart, even if it was just one night—then he had to take one, too. To show her the real him. She bit his lip. Hard.

He jerked away. "What the hell?" His hand tangled again, twisting in her hair, pulling her head back.

Yes. She arched against him, her nipples pebbling, her breath catching. More. She wanted more of him.

His eyes glittered a dangerous blue in the dim light, a clear warning glowing there.

A knock on the door had him off her and grabbing his gun, his boxer-briefs clearly showing his arousal. "What?"

"Had a sighting on the kid and teacher," Raider called through the door. "We need to hit the road as fast as possible. Be out in ten."

Hunter's shoulders went down, and he turned to look at her over his shoulder. "It's probably for the best."

It sure as heck didn't feel like it.

Chapter Eight

Hunter led the way toward Fred's Convenience store, a brick building with bright yellow trim located in central South Dakota. His senses shut down the second the metallic smell of blood hit him. He instantly flashed back to a knife fight he'd barely won.

Raider and Wolfe flanked him, and Faye was right behind them. He turned, brushed past the other two, and took Faye's arm to pull her around and back onto the sidewalk in front of the store. Emergency vehicles filled the newly asphalted parking lot, their red and blue lights swirling against a pretty spring sky, this one devoid of clouds. The police had done a good job of cordoning off the area with yellow crime tape, but small crowds had gathered on the other side, people craning their necks to see the macabre. A news van screeched to a stop at the corner.

Faye halted, turning to look up at him. "What?"

"I'd like for you to stay outside," he said, scanning the crowd for any threats. It was unlikely Louise would return to the store, but he couldn't leave Faye outside without knowing for sure.

"Excuse me, folks." A sixty-something sheriff in uniform approached them, his gray hair buzz-cut short and his eyes a shrewd brown. "Show me some ID, please." His gait was casual, but he moved like a guy who could handle himself.

Ah, shit. They didn't have any identification.

Raider instantly appeared and flashed a badge. "Raider Tanaka, Homeland Defense Department."

"Sheriff Lodi," the sheriff said, his gaze narrowing. "What does HDD want with a convenience store robbery?"

Raider smiled, his clean-shaven jaw making him look like any good Fed. "We're helping the FBI out with this one. It's a kidnapping and crime spree across state lines." He glanced at his watch. "My unit commander should be landing in town in about an hour, and he has more paperwork for you if you want it."

The sheriff looked them over. "All right. I did receive a fax from HDD in DC and just wanted to double check. We're finished processing the scene, if you want to take a look. The kidnapping victim is a minor?"

Hunter nodded.

The sheriff shook his head. "That's just terrible. I'll have my men start canvassing the neighborhood, and we'll have our techs send the evidence to your lab. The fax gave me a contact person. Your lab will be much quicker than ours. Trust me." He turned and started barking orders at some patrolmen standing over by their cars.

"Nice guy," Faye said.

"Yes." Hunter kept his voice level, even though his gut ached. "Stay out here, Faye. I'll be back in a minute."

She pulled her arm free. "No. I'm acting as a psychologist on this case. Maybe seeing the crime scene will be helpful."

Maybe? Not in a million years. She'd experienced too much violence as a young girl, and he knew for a fact she'd never seen a crime scene like this one. When her patient had killed himself, she hadn't been informed until a week later, so she hadn't witnessed the scene. He wasn't going to let her be haunted by this. "There's no need for you to see anything." Or smell the blood or experience the hollow air left by recent death. "We'll tell you what happened."

Her face screwed up as if she was going to argue with him, something she'd always done well.

He waved the sheriff back over. "Hey, sheriff. This is our shrink, and she's not cleared for crime scenes. Put her in the back of a squad car if you need to." Without waiting for an answer, he turned and walked into the store, ready to take the heat from her later. At the moment, his head hurt, his gut ached, and he probably had blue balls from being settled against her sweet body earlier that morning.

She sputtered, but the sheriff had already herded her toward a patrolman who looked like Thor. "You can speak with Deputy Latham. He was first on the scene, and he'll tell you everything you want to know," the sheriff said as they walked away.

Hunter turned and forced himself to walk into the crime scene. Blood splatter covered the wall behind the counter and cash register, while a stack of potato chip bags had been toppled, with several spilling chips onto the floor, now stained an ominous red. He leaned over the counter to see a blood pool.

"Owner was a guy named Fred Fredrickson," Raider said, reading from a crime report somebody must've handed him. "Was thirty years old, lived in Brookeville his entire life, married five years. No kids." Raider gestured down an aisle of cleaning supplies. "Second victim. Forty-year-old Marla Jones. Nurse, not married, had a basket full of the makings for nachos, as well as two bottles of wine."

Marla wasn't going to make it to her party tonight. "Dead?"

"No. In surgery, having three bullets removed. Chances aren't good." Raider looked up, his gaze dark. "We're getting the video footage now. Could be one shooter—easy."

Or Hunter's brother might've joined in the killing. A rock rolled over in his stomach. If Jackson had killed, there wasn't a lot Hunter could do to help him. "When do we get the video?"

"It's already gone to our operative in DC, and she'll have an answer soon," Raider said, an odd infliction in his tone.

She, huh? Hunter would have to figure that one out later. He steeled his shoulders and walked down the aisle to find blood and materials used by the paramedics to save Marla's life. Images and smells and sounds hit him so hard and fast, he grabbed a shelf and just stood.

"You okay?" Wolfe asked, coming out of nowhere.

"Yeah." Hunter straightened and forced all expression off his face.

Wolfe nodded, petting the kitten in his pocket. "Been there. Still there sometimes." With the cryptic remark that somehow made perfect sense, he turned and strode away.

Hunter finished surveying the scene, keeping more flashbacks at bay. Then he turned to leave the crime scene and deal with a no doubt pissed off Faye—never an enjoyable moment.

Except now, after having touched her this morning, he wanted to take her down to the ground after they fought. And he didn't really want to be gentle this time.

* * * *

Faye sat at the table on the patio of the sports bar, flanked by Hunter and Raider and facing Wolfe. They had two pitchers of Hefeweizen in front of them as well as full glasses, although Faye had opted for a Pepsi. She didn't judge Hunter for drinking beer. He should have it if he wanted it. As a guy in control all the time, he'd never let alcohol take over his life, unlike either of their fathers.

Hunter had insisted upon the outside table, and his face slowly lost its pinched look as he drank the beer and let the afternoon sun beam down on them. A nice spring breeze filled with the scents of phlox and peonies wafted through, providing a sense of peace.

Wolfe quietly fed Kat, his gaze on his beer, while Raider typed on his smartphone—all business.

The crime scene must've been bad. Even so, she was part of this team, and they'd had no right to make her stay outside. "You guys can't do that again. Leave me out."

Hunter's eyes darkened. "We're all military or police force, Brown Eyed Girl. You aren't, and you never have been. There is exactly zero reason for you to see a crime scene like that one."

Raider nodded as he typed. "Agreed."

Wolfe looked her over, glanced at the other two men, and then shrugged. "I'm staying out of it, although I think Brown Eyed Girl would be a lovely last name for you, since you're looking for a unique one."

Faye sighed.

Wolfe straightened. "You're not a shrink any longer?"

"No." Her ears heated. "I'm looking at a different career."

"Like what?" He fed more crackers to the kitten.

She pressed a thumb into her opposite palm to relax. "Maybe landscape design?" The idea had definitely taken root.

He grinned. "I have a house. A real one."

She bit her lip. "I haven't gone to school yet."

"That's okay. You should come look at it anyway." Wolfe patted the kitten.

Hunter cut him a look.

A trio of young women, maybe around twenty years old, giggled as they shared another pitcher of margaritas. A brunette wearing jeans with red high heels kept giving Hunter a look. A "hey baby" look.

Faye barely kept from glaring at her. Who wore red high heels and jeans to lunch? Seriously.

Raider stopped typing, watched his screen, and sighed. "Video came in." He took a big drink of his beer before setting down the mug and looking directly at Hunter. "Good news is that the kid wasn't at this robbery. Bad news is that the clerk behind the counter offered up the money, didn't fight, and Louise Stockley shot him anyway. She's definitely on a killing spree."

Faye caught her breath and sat back. "That could be disastrous if Jackson disagrees with her or stops following her lead." She bit her lip, trying to remember the one class on abnormal psychology she'd taken years ago. "She'd see that as a betrayal." And probably kill the kid.

Hunter sat back in his chair, flipping through the manila file that Dana had given them. "Dana did a good job on this."

Wolfe leaned forward. "Speaking of Dana, the very lovely journalist. She's single, right? I can see us together."

Did he ever have a thought he didn't share? Faye let the sun warm her back. "She did say you were cute."

"I'm effing adorable," Wolfe agreed.

Hunter rolled his eyes. "The background Dana found on Louise showed she spent summers at a couple of camps; one in northern Idaho and the other eastern Washington. Maybe she's heading back there."

Faye took a sip of her soda. "Could be. She might be trying to take Jackson to a place and time where she felt safe. Where childhood was good."

"That's screwed up, considering they're together," Wolfe said, downing his mug in one long drink. He leaned over to refill his glass.

Tension pricked Faye's neck, and her breath quickened, but she kept her hand steady on the glass.

Even so, Wolfe cocked his head to the side and studied her, his eyes dark. "I'm never out of control. I could drink both of these pitchers and the entire keg out back and at no time would you know it. More important, I would never harm a woman. No matter how much I drink, you not for a moment need to fear me." He pushed the mug away. "And if you ask me to stop drinking right now, I will."

It was the most serious she'd seen him. Her heart warmed toward the soldier. "It was an old reaction, and I don't need you to stop drinking the beer. But thank you for offering."

He grinned. "Good. I'm still thirsty."

Hunter set his hand at the base of her neck and kneaded her nape, soothing all the tension just the way he used to do. She closed her eyes and nearly groaned, feeling her muscles slowly unwind. It was such a natural gesture that it took her a few moments to remember they didn't do this anymore. But it felt so good, she didn't protest.

The thumping of helicopter blades forced her eyelids open. Hunter released her and leaned back. She looked up to see a battered and dented helicopter with faded green paint set down in the middle of the parking lot and bounce twice.

Raider groaned. "Now, that's a piece of shit."

Faye swallowed. This was the helicopter for Raider's unit? She'd been expecting a Blackhawk, something badass and sleek. Not a rusting deathtrap. "Why do I have the feeling you haven't told us everything about your deep ops unit?"

Wolfe sighed. "We kind of suck. Well, not really. We're super smart, and we solve cases nobody else solves, but the HDD doesn't exactly like us, so our resources aren't that great."

Raider nodded, his gaze sober. "We're lucky to have that helicopter."

The vehicle powered down, and the pilot's door opened. A massive German Shepherd leaped out, barked twice, and made a beeline for them, easily clearing the iron fence between the tables and the parking lot.

Then everything happened too fast to react. Both Wolfe and Raider jumped up, reaching for the pitchers of beer. The dog hit the table, skidded across the wood, and reached the first pitcher before either man could snag it. He stuck his nose in the beer, growling and drinking so quickly the alcohol was half gone before Raider could wrestle the pitcher away. "Roscoe, stop it," he snapped.

Roscoe lifted his furry head, barked once, and executed a shockingly graceful half-circle leap to land on the nearest table, his beer-coated head dropping into the margarita pitcher with total abandon. The three women yelped and scooted back from the table as he slurped down the entire strawberry blended liquid.

He lifted his head and licked his fur, his mouth widening in what could only be considered a doggy smile.

Faye pressed her hand to her chest. "What in the world?"

"Goddamn it, Roscoe," bellowed a man who jumped down from the helicopter. He had shaggy black hair, piercing green eyes, and an angled face that would be truly intriguing if it wasn't so pissed off.

Roscoe lost the grin, whined, and leaped beneath the table to lick one woman's ankles. She giggled and kicked off her heels. The dog instantly stuck his front feet in the red shoes and clopped out from under the table, grinning again.

Raider dropped his chin to his chest. "Faye? Hunter? Meet Roscoe. Our unit mascot."

"He's a drunk," Hunter said slowly, crossing his arms, his mouth still slightly open. "And he likes high heels?"

"He thinks he's too short," the new guy said, halting on the other side of the fence. "Roscoe? You're grounded," he called out, his voice a harsh growl.

These people were insane. Faye moved her chair slightly away from the new guy, who had a truly deadly glint in his eyes.

Raider sighed. "Faye and Hunter? Meet Angus Force. Our boss."

Chapter Nine

Hunter finished his fish and chips, drinking water instead of the rest of his beer. The heels had been returned to the woman wearing the too-tight jeans, and Angus Force had bought that table another round of margaritas, so everyone was happy. Especially the dog snoring beneath the table with his furry head on Faye's tennis shoes. "Are you sure we shouldn't take him to a vet? Alcohol kills dogs."

Force wiped his mouth after finishing his steak. "Nope. I've taken him several times after he's done something like this, and the vet says Roscoe has the liver of an old miner. We can't explain it, so we just try to keep him away from the booze. Sorry about this time. He got out of the helicopter way too fast."

Hunter studied Force. He didn't like Raider being in a dangerous unit, and yet...there was something worthwhile there. Something off the wall and uncontrolled that might be good for him. And wasn't there a comment earlier about a woman? He should get to the bottom of that.

Force drank down some beer. "I need you back, Wolfe. Today." He gave Raider a look. "You can have as much time as you need for this, but we might have to go forward with the Irish Op without you."

Hunter's interest was piqued, and he took a drink of his water, watching the interchange play out.

"No," Raider said. "She doesn't go without me. That's a deal breaker, Force."

Interesting.

Faye leaned forward. "Just who is 'she'?"

Leave it to Faye to ask the question. Man, sometimes Hunter adored her.

"Nobody," Raider said, which meant the direct opposite of "nobody."

"Wolfe?" Faye asked, turning her prettiest smile on the soldier.

Smart. Freaking brilliant. Hunter hid a smile as he studied Wolfe.

The man's ears turned red. "Brigid is our computer hacker. She's insanely intelligent, and—"

"Enough," Force said, his voice firm. "We can't discuss undercover work."

Faye turned to Raider. "You are not going undercover. Absolutely not."

Angus Force frowned. "Why not?"

Faye pressed her lips together and crossed her arms. Oh, she'd never betray Raider. Hunter cut his brother a quick look. Just how much of his experience had he shared with this new unit of his?

Force looked at the two of them. "Why do I get the feeling I'm missing something?"

"You're not," Raider said quietly. "My family is just being overprotective, which is their duty and their right. But they need to butt out and now."

Wolfe finished his beer. "I can go undercover with Brigid. We'd make a nice couple, if you ask me. Opposites attract and all that."

"Opposites?" Raider snapped. "You're exactly alike. You're both stubborn, crazy as shit, total rebels. There's nothing opposite about you." He downed half of his beer, his hand steady on the glass, tension sparking the air around him. "You both require a calming influence, whether you realize it or not."

Whoa. That was a lot of emotion from Raider Tanaka. Hunter kicked back in his chair, studying his brother. Was there something about this Brigid? "I'd really like to meet this woman."

"Me too," Faye said, reaching down to pet the dog between his ears. He snuffled in pure contentment. "Tell us more about her, Wolfe."

Wolfe looked at Raider, seemed to think it over, and then shook his head. "Not my place." He scratched his elbow. "And I don't need a calming influence. I'm calm. Always calm." He even said the words calmly. "I've found ways to exist in this world. Lattes help, so long as they have sprinkles. The sprinkles make all the difference."

Lattes and sprinkles? Hunter really wanted into this guy's head. It was impossible to determine whether Wolfe was serious or just messing with all of them. Or somehow both.

Angus gave Raider a look that promised a later discussion before drawing out a folded map and pen from his back pocket. "It looks like your perps were traveling along Interstate 40 and have now moved to parallel Interstate 90, taking back roads." He drew a line along the roads. "Louise, at least, is hitting convenience stores and small restaurants out of the way but still along the route."

Faye nodded. "I've conducted a comparison of the places Louise has robbed so far. All small, not part of any chain. Mom-and-pop-type places."

"Could be just because many of those don't have up-to-date security," Hunter said, his attention caught as Kat jumped out of Wolfe's pocket and hit the ground. He straightened to save the kitten from the dog, but nobody else moved.

Wolfe looked down. "Kat likes Roscoe. They're buddies."

Hunter angled his head to see better, and sure enough, Kat jumped on top of Roscoe's back, dug in his claws, and settled down for a nap. Roscoe didn't even twitch or open his eyes. Freaking weird. All of them.

Faye studied the map. "I'm thinking Louise is just being smart, but in that background information from Dana, it does say that

Louise grew up in a small town where her father was a mechanic. Let's get some info on her mother. I doubt it has anything to do with locally owned stores, but let's double check."

"I'll take care of it," Force said, standing up. "Wolfe? We have to go."

Wolfe snagged the kitten with one hand and slid him into his pocket before standing. He looked at Raider. "You need me, you call me."

Raider nodded. "Ditto."

It was nice to see Raider had found a place. The place might be a disaster, but Hunter would solve that later. Then Wolfe looked at him. "You think Dana would go out with me? I've never dated a journalist."

Hunter shrugged. "I don't know. You could always ask her, I guess."

Wolfe smiled big before focusing on Faye. "You're Raider's, so you're ours now, too. Call, and we'll come running." He looked over at the dilapidated helicopter. "Probably. I mean, we might die in that thing first." With that, he bounded over the fence and strode away, not looking back.

Angus Force nudged his dog with one boot. "I'd better get to the helicopter before Wolfe decides he wants to pilot it. Roscoe. Move, now."

The dog groaned, stood, and licked Faye's hand before turning and leaping over the fence as gracefully as had Wolfe.

Force rolled his eyes, clapped Raider on the back, nodded at the rest of them, calmly opened the gate nobody else had bothered to use, and headed for the helicopter.

Raider sighed. "It's amazing any of us are still alive."

Wasn't that the truth? Hunter looked at the map. "On that note, let's get on the road."

* * * *

Faye stretched out in Raider's rented SUV as Hunter drove and Raider worked his phone, coordinating with federal agencies from the passenger seat. They were somewhere in South Dakota. She flipped on the overhead light as nighttime fell again. Frustration tormented her. There were too many small convenience stores and restaurants along I-90 to even guess which one Louise would hit next. Why was she killing people when she didn't have to?

Faye spread out the pictures of the victims so far. Men and women—all different ages. There wasn't a pattern. Louise was just killing to kill.

That was a pattern.

"This isn't what I studied in school," Faye mused, reading over another hospital report.

"We'll have a profile from my unit's shrink in a couple of hours," Raider said, looking over his shoulder. "But I don't think there's much we haven't figured out already. Louise had a bad childhood, a bad marriage, and she's trying to recapture a happy time by using Jackson."

Yeah, that about summed it up. "She's robbing for money and killing for pleasure," Faye said, shaking her head. "It's rare for a woman to be a serial killer, but she's getting off on the power." Which meant that she'd felt helpless a lot in her young life. None of that, however, was an excuse for killing, or committing statutory rape. "You all know this doesn't end well, right?"

Hunter nodded, his hands steady on the steering wheel. "We'll try to bring her in alive. If she lets us."

Faye was more concerned with Jackson being brought in alive. By the tightening of Hunter's shoulders, so was he. Just how far would Jackson go for the woman? "Jackson's mother died young, and he's probably never really had a maternal presence in his life," Faye said quietly. "He was only with Miss Angelina for a day, and by that time, he was already entrenched with Louise. The hold she has on him is hard to understand, but it's there and it's solid." She had to give Hunter some type of warning to prepare him.

"I'm aware," Hunter said, his blue gaze meeting hers in the rearview mirror. "But nobody shoots at that kid. Got it?" He looked to his side.

Raider nodded, not looking up from his phone. "Copy that. We duck and cover if Jackson comes out shooting. But chances are we won't be the only law enforcement to arrive if there's a showdown. We can't control what other cops do."

Hunter's hands tightened, and the steering wheel protested with a slight squeak. "We have to get to him before anybody else does."

To do that, they had to find the kid. "There doesn't seem to be a recurring time interval between robberies," Faye said. No set time, or even ritual that she could see. "The only pattern is that the robberies are becoming more frequent. She's escalating instead of taking time to enjoy whatever money she takes."

Which meant Louise liked the act of robbing more than the spoils. That didn't bode well for Jackson Holt.

Hunter increased the speed of the vehicle as they headed for the next small town. "Do you suppose there's any way Jackson is innocent in this?"

Faye bit her lip. "Since he's not at the crime scenes, it's possible he doesn't know the extent of the bloodshed." She really wanted to reassure him, but she wouldn't lie. "There's no way he's unaware that Louise is robbing to get money." Did that make him an accessory? Probably. But they'd deal with the legal ramifications later. Right now, they just needed to save the kid's life. Hunter couldn't live with the guilt if his half-brother died so young. She knew Hunter, and the burden he already carried was unimaginable.

This would destroy him.

She should've been there for him before, but she'd had her own tragedy to deal with. Then Mark had died. But now, she could help Hunter. Even if it made her vulnerable, and even if it got her heart broken again. She could be there for him and help him through this.

Hunter's phone dinged, and he pressed a button. "What?"

"It's Wolfe. A call just came in from Ferris City reporting a robbery in progress."

Hunter swore. "We just passed that town." He flipped an illegal U-turn, bumping the vehicle across the grassy area between the interstate's west and eastbound lanes, and headed east. "We might get there in time." He clicked off and sped up, passing a semi that honked in protest.

Wolfe gave the address over the speaker and a quick set of directions off the interstate.

Faye's breath caught, and she unbuckled her seatbelt so she could exit from the car quickly.

Raider took his gun out from his holster and reached into the jockey box for Hunter's heavy black gun. He handed it over.

Hunter took the off ramp and ran a stop sign at the bottom, not slowing down.

"Force told the locals you were Feds and not to shoot you when you barreled into the middle of everything. Call me afterward," Wolfe said, disengaging the call.

Hunter took another fast left, and the tires squealed but stayed on the ground. "Faye? You get down and stay down. I'm going to have to drive up to the front."

No way. If there was a chance to talk Louise or even Jackson down, she was the only person with a minimal amount of training. She'd save Hunter's brother if she could, and she had at least an idea of how to connect with Louise. But she didn't argue. Just waited for Hunter to slam to a stop in front of a brick building with "Clara's Convenience Store" lit up in bright blue lights.

Two police cars already flanked the parking lot, their lights on, the officers crouched behind their doors with guns pointed at the store.

Hunter and Raider jumped out, and Faye followed—whether they wanted her to or not. She had to save that kid.

Chapter Ten

Hunter swung open his door and crouched outside the vehicle, his gun out. Apparently Force had gotten through to the locals, because nobody moved his way or tried to shoot him. He could see Raider taking up a similar position on the other side of the vehicle. "Status?" he called out.

"Hostage situation," the nearest cop, a kid still looking fresh and pressed, confirmed. "The owner, Clara, is in there for sure. We saw her before she drew the blinds."

"How many perps?" Hunter asked, his gut whirling. God, he hoped Jackson wasn't in there.

The cop looked over, blue eyes wide. "We just saw one. A woman—the one that has been on the news."

Good. Maybe Jackson wasn't there. But he could've just been out of sight.

"We don't have a hostage negotiator, and the chief is out of town," the kid said, his hand shaking slightly on his gun. "You're Feds, right?"

"I can negotiate." Faye stepped up, her face so pale that the fine blue veins beneath her skin showed through.

Hunter yanked her down behind him. "Get back in the car. Now."

"No." She plastered her hand to his lower back. "I'm the only one with a modicum of training here. It wasn't with hostages, but I worked with patients…" Her voice trailed off.

Hunter closed his eyes. What had happened with her patient wasn't her fault. Nobody truly knew what lived in another person's mind.

The young cop tossed over a bullhorn. "We don't have anybody here with hostage experience."

Damn it. Hunter caught it easily. His entire military career had been geared toward understanding the target in order to find and shoot him. Not to negotiate or forge a bond. Raider was better with people, but he also aimed to arrest or take down. Negotiation, especially with hostages, was a whole different skill set, and having a psychology degree would certainly help. But if Faye tried to assist, and things went south, she'd go to that dark place again. How could he let her do that?

Faye reached around him and took the bullhorn, clicking the button. "Louise? My name is Faye, and I'd really like to talk to you."

Nothing. No sound came from within.

Faye looked over at the kid. "Tell me about Clara. What do you know?"

"Everything," the cop said, the swirling lights dancing across his clean-shaven face. He had short black hair, dark skin, and sober brown eyes. "Everyone knows everybody around here. Clara is about seventy years old. Lost her husband in Vietnam and raised two kids by herself. Married an asshole the second time around and nearly took his head off with a frying pan. He's long gone."

"Where are her kids?" Faye whispered.

"One's a doctor in town, and the other is a stage actor in New York. He comes home every holiday, though."

Faye nodded and partially stood, clicking the button again. "Louise? That Clara you're holding has had a rough life, too. Married the wrong guy and had a frying pan incident."

There was silence, and then the blind slats opened.

Faye tried to move out from behind Hunter, but he shook his head. If she moved too far, he'd toss her butt back in the vehicle, whether she liked it or not.

The door slowly opened. "Get the cops out of here, or I'll shoot her." Louise pushed Clara in front of her, using her as a shield. She had a handgun pressed to the elderly woman's throat.

Clara's gray hair was in a ponytail, and her brown eyes were calm. Her shoulders were hunched with age beneath her flowered dress, but she held herself well, and was at least five inches taller than Louise, unfortunately. She made a good shield. Her pale skin was papery thin, and she looked like everyone's idea of a sweet grandmother. So far, Hunter didn't have a shot.

Faye moved slightly to the side and Hunter tensed. "How could you shoot somebody who's had bad experiences like you have? Her husband hurt her, and she hurt him back and then left him. Your husband is a bad guy, too, right?"

Louise barely leaned around Clara, her eyes wild. She wore jeans, boots, and a black sweatshirt. "You don't know me. Don't even try to get into my head."

"I don't want in your head," Faye said. "I just want everyone to get out of this alive."

The smile Louise flashed gave Hunter the chills. "None of us gets out of this world alive. You should know that." She cocked her head, her gaze landing on Hunter. "You look…familiar."

"Jackson Holt is my brother," Hunter said, standing in front of Faye again. "Just found out about him. Had no clue."

"Right," Louise said, drawing back, her nostrils flaring. "You left him with that asshole who hurt him. If you'd found out, you would've just hurt that boy more. I know men like you."

"No, you don't," Hunter countered, lowering his gun. "I've never hurt a woman. Not once. And I never would."

Louise laughed, the sound high and crazed. "That's what you all say. 'I'm sorry I hurt you. It'll never happen again.' Or even worse, 'That never happened.' So much bullshit." She pulled Clara back a couple of feet.

Faye leaned around Hunter. "Why convenience stores, Louise? I mean, I understand why you love Jackson." To her credit, she didn't let her disgust show. "But why do you keep killing people in small stores? Your parents didn't own one, did they?"

"No. My parents didn't do shit," Louise said slowly.

Okay. Something had definitely happened. Hunter let Faye keep the lead.

"It's not this woman's fault," Faye said. "She's a nice lady who lost her first husband and then left one who hurt her. She's like you."

Louise pressed the gun harder against Clara's thin throat, and the elderly woman winced. "Leave this parking lot, or I shoot her in the head," Louise bellowed. The door closed, and the locks engaged.

"Shit," Hunter muttered.

"I don't think Jackson is in there," Faye whispered.

Neither did Hunter. How the hell was he going to save Clara? He took the bullhorn and clicked the button. "Louise? You have three minutes. Come out and we'll help you. If you make us come in, you won't live to see Jackson again." It was all he had to bargain with.

One minute passed. Then another. A shot echoed, and then an old truck zoomed through the alley outside, heading down the dirt road.

Hunter jumped into the front seat, waited until the other two got in, and then raced behind the police cars. They were going to catch this psychopath.

* * * *

Faye knocked her head against the back seat of the SUV as they came to yet another dirt road that led in three different directions. After shooting the officer guarding the back door of the store, Louise had stolen Clara's old truck. The elderly lady was in the passenger seat. Unfortunately, the back alley led to a fence that Louise had managed to lock with a padlock kept there.

It had taken ten way-too-precious moments for the police to find bolt cutters.

Roads climbed the mountains in every direction, and they'd been searching for well over two hours, keeping in communication with the other police officers, as well as civilian volunteers that both Hunter and Raider had argued against including.

The county cops hadn't listened.

The locals probably did know the mountains much better than anybody else, but Louise wouldn't hesitate to shoot. Was Clara still alive? Faye wiped her forehead. What if something she'd said had gotten the lady killed?

"You did an excellent job," Hunter said, reading her mind as usual. He moved his head, scanning the area around the narrow road, which had a mountain rising on one side and a drop-off on the other. "Finding similarities between the two women definitely helped."

Raider kept reading his phone. "All right. More information from our source. Turns out that Louise had a summer job at a convenience store throughout junior high. She quit suddenly once she started high school, but there's no mention of why." He kept reading. "Ah. The owner was a guy named Burt Samms, and he ran the store with his wife, Velda. Burt was later accused of molesting a neighborhood girl, but no charges were brought."

Well. That was that, then. Faye shook her head. "So Louise, since she's just abandoned her life in general, is now out to make all convenience store owners in small towns pay?" The logic was twisted, but serial killers didn't need reasons that made sense to anybody else.

"Where does that leave Jackson?" Hunter switched on his high beams to better illuminate the forest.

Who knew. Louise was unstable, but she cared about Jackson in her twisted way, so hopefully he would be safe until they could reach him. But how in the world was it possible he didn't know about the violence?

Something among the trees caught her eye. "Hey. Wait a second."

Hunter slowed down. Then he stopped and jumped out of the SUV, running for a stumbling Clara as she emerged from the trees. He caught the older woman and lifted her, carrying her to the vehicle.

Faye threw open the door and scooted over, yanking a blanket from the back.

Clara patted Hunter's chest. "My, you're strong." He set her down gently.

Faye covered her with the blanket and gently removed branches from her hair. "We'll get you to a hospital."

Hunter ran around to the driver's seat, jumped in, and gunned the engine while Raider quickly called in the report.

Clara smoothed her wrinkled hands over the blanket. "I don't need a doctor, young lady. I'm just fine." She pulled another twig out of her hair. "Although I sure would like my truck back, if anybody has found it yet. It was my first husband, Earl's, you know."

"I didn't know." Faye studied the woman. Bright eyes, good breathing, no shaking. She seemed all right. "Can you tell us what happened?"

"Oh." Clara shook her head. "That woman was as crazy as an outhouse rat."

Faye made sure the blanket was tucked around the woman. "Yet you stayed alive. You did good."

"That's because of you." Clara reached a gnarled hand to pat Faye's, her palm cold. "Got me to talking about my crappy second marriage, and she related. Said she found a good man now, though."

Faye winced. "Did she say anything about this new man?"

"Nope. Just that he supported her completely and would love her forever." Clara shivered. "Sad girl, honest. But she only has one oar in the water, if you know what I mean."

Hunter swung the car around, headed toward town. "Did she say where the man is, or where they're going next?"

Clara settled back in the seat, her dirty tennis shoes on the rubber mat. "Just that they were heading somewhere safe where they could live off the land. Not sure what she meant about the land, considering she cleaned me out." Clara drew a twenty-dollar bill from her pocket. "But she gave me this back so I had some money for a taxi." Her gray eyebrows wrinkled. "We're a small town. Don't even have taxis."

Perhaps there was some sort of hope for Louise. Faye wanted to think so. "Did Louise indicate that the, ah, man she talked about, knew about these robberies?"

Clara shrugged a bony shoulder. "No. But when she first came in and pointed the gun at me, she did mention that she couldn't get blood on her clothes, so she asked me to back up to the far side of the counter."

Chills slid down Faye's back. "I'm so sorry that happened to you."

Raider turned around. "Did you back up?"

"Gracious, no. I moved toward her," Clara said, nodding emphatically. "Figured if she shot me, she deserved to wear my blood."

Faye shivered, impressed and alarmed at the same time. "Good for you."

Clara patted her hand again. "You all need to be careful. She seemed awfully determined to protect this boyfriend from you, Hunter. I heard you give your name to her, and she didn't like it. Said she'd make sure you never saw either of them again."

Chapter Eleven

Hunter finger-combed his wet hair after his shower, drawing his jeans back on and leaving his chest bare. His tattoo looked even darker than usual. Was Faye's still delicate and beautiful against her pretty skin? He was sure it would always be that way.

His body hurt, his temples pounded, and his temper was ready to roar. They'd taken Clara to the hospital against her wishes, and her daughter the doctor had been there, so Hunter had felt all right leaving.

Then they'd driven west until they couldn't drive any longer, finally finding yet another fleabag motel to stay the night. This one had several available rooms, so he'd gotten three, wishing there had only been two. But losing himself in Faye right now, in her delightfully curvy body, wouldn't be fair to either one of them. And there was no way he could sleep platonically next to her for another night.

Ever since the first time he'd met her, when they were just kids, he'd wanted to be special to her.

Why the hell had he given up that dream? He was a fighter, but he'd been too screwed up to fight for the one thing, the one person, who truly mattered in his life.

He stepped out of the bathroom just as a knock came at the door. The rough carpet scratched his bare feet as he walked past the dark blue bedspread and opened the door, expecting an update from Raider.

Faye stood in the moonlight dressed in yoga pants and a T-shirt, her hair wet and her pretty face scrubbed clean.

All words deserted him.

She shifted, her movements uncharacteristically nervous. "Raider got a report. The cop Louise shot is going to be okay."

Relief filtered through the raw awareness grabbing Hunter around the throat. "Good." He looked both ways down the deserted walkway and then out to the quiet parking lot. "I'll walk you back to your room."

"I don't want my room." She placed both hands on his bare abdomen and pushed him back inside.

His mind shut down. Just one little touch from her and his body went from slow burn to wild inferno. "I can't sleep next to you tonight. Can't do it." How could she not understand that? She pushed him again, and he backed up, wanting her touch more than anything in the world. "Faye."

She shut the door. "Then sleep under me. On top of me. Inside me."

His mouth went dry. Hope and want and need attacked him so quickly, his hands reached for her when his mind knew better.

She stretched up onto her tiptoes and pressed her sweet mouth against his.

He groaned low, letting her kiss him for the briefest of moments. Then he took over. Unable to help himself, he kissed her hard, knowing her taste. Wanting it more than he wanted his next breath. She tasted of honey and wildness and everything sweet in the world. Of desire and trust and even the faintest hint of a chocolate milkshake she'd had before they'd found their rooms.

It wasn't enough. It'd never be enough. He slid a hand up her soft neck and pressed his thumb against her jaw, forcing her to open her mouth. To let him in. He'd tried to warn her. To let her have some space. To keep her safe and untouched and happy with the memories of them.

He couldn't be the same guy he'd been at eighteen. Even at twenty-five. He'd seen too much. Hell, he'd done too much. But for now, just this moment, he let himself drown in her taste.

She moaned, leaning into him, her mouth so soft. It was like she'd shocked him with a taser, shooting sparks down his spine to land hard in his cock. God, he wanted her. Almost too much. He released her jaw to slide his fingers deep into her wet hair, remembering the softness he'd dreamed about while fighting worlds away. So far away.

He tightened his fingers into a fist, pulling back her head, swallowing her gasp of surprise.

That sound. That simple and sweet sound should've stopped him. Should've made him remember why it was safer to keep her away from him. A decent guy would stop right now.

He'd stopped being a decent guy a million years ago. She'd come to his room. She'd kissed him. It was too late for him to talk her out of it. He pushed his tongue deeper into her mouth, kissing her harder, taking them both higher than was probably sane.

She shuddered, her nipples pebbling against his chest. He needed to see those. Without losing a beat, he ripped her shirt over her head. Then he dropped his, nibbling and sucking at her full breasts, his hand at her hair, keeping her in place. She tried to pull free, her mouth wild on his neck, but he held her where he wanted her. Her legs wobbled against his, and the scent of her desire nearly dropped him to his knees.

Her helpless sigh, full of need, only spurred him on.

He reached for her yoga pants, and her hands were there first, shoving them down her legs faster than he could. He smiled against her breast and gently bit.

She stilled. All of her.

Yeah. He lifted his head, his gaze pinning hers. "When I want you to move, I'll tell you."

Her pupils contracted. He sensed her spirit and defiance and so much need he could feel it in his own bones. This was what he'd tried to shield her from. The creamy skin of her face had flushed a lovely pink, her mouth a deep red.

"Is that a fact?" Her voice was so low and hoarse, the sound shooting right down to his cock.

"Yes. See why this is a bad idea?" he asked, his voice rougher than glass crunching across asphalt.

Her jaw firmed. Ah shit. He knew that look. Her chin lowered, her eyes wide and direct. "I'm not afraid of you, Hunter. Never have been and never will be. So you just go right ahead and show me what you've got, tough guy."

The challenge. She knew exactly what she was doing, damn her. So he stood, plucked her right off the ground, tossed her on the bed, and followed her down.

* * * *

His eyes were different. A darkness, an intensity lived there that she'd never seen. She couldn't look away, and a heated electric spark shot straight through her. "You're not afraid of me?" His voice held a deceptive softness that made her tremble, but not with anything close to fear. "You want me to show you what I've got?" The mild tone, said with such raw control, nearly sent her into an early orgasm.

"Yes," she whispered, meaning it. All of it.

He moved over her, all rough muscle and graceful edge. He'd told her to back away, and she hadn't.

Her entire life, she'd been conditioned to heed a warning. Any woman with half a brain would walk away from a guy who warned her off.

But she couldn't leave Hunter. Not even now, when he was struggling so desperately for control. He was afraid of losing it. She wasn't. She could handle him in any state—even wounded and pissed, which he was at the moment.

The atmosphere swelled, and he settled himself against her panties, his cock hard though his jeans. A sense of danger, of barely leashed violence, thumped from him. Oh, she knew he'd never physically hurt her. Not in a million years. This was a threat of a totally different kind—one that reached down inside her and made her ache with a force she'd never be able to explain. She was feeling every pulsing beat, and she couldn't put it into words.

So be it.

He somehow moved and wrapped his fingers around both of her wrists, pinning them on either side of her hips. Then he ground against her, and the delicious friction nearly made her eyes roll back. "You don't know what you're playing with, Faye."

No, she didn't. But she wanted more. And she was fairly certain she wasn't playing. Even as a kid of eighteen, the first time they'd made love, she'd known it was a risk beyond what most people understood. That she'd never want to be free of him. That she'd always want to belong to him.

But then, he'd known he was leaving for the military soon. He'd always held something back. He'd returned darker and more wounded. She leaned up and kissed the tattoo above his right bicep. The one of the Celtic knot with four angles that matched hers.

"Faye." The way he said her name... Then he kissed her, his body trapping hers, his hands easily pinning hers to the bed. "There's too much going on right now for this to make sense." His lips moved against hers, his gaze so close she could see gold flecks within the blue of his eyes. "I want you, but we'll have to figure out us later." The tension in him ratcheted up, and she could feel even the muscles in his hips tighten.

"I know," she said, realizing with a bone-deep instinct that he already possessed much more of her than he'd ever understood. But he was wrong. They should figure them out as soon as possible. What they were about to do would just cement the knowledge in him. The craving for that, the hunger for him to hold her as closely inside himself as she had always kept him, uncoiled deep inside her. There was something she wanted to say, but she couldn't find the words.

He kissed her again, holding her hands, his chest hard as rock against her breasts. So much heat and power. She licked his bottom lip, squirming against him. "You're wearing too many clothes," she gasped.

He grinned, and the shadows in his eyes finally fled. Releasing her hands, he unbuttoned his jeans. She frantically helped shove them down, along with her panties.

Then they were skin to skin. She closed her eyes and breathed in, memories assailing her. God, she'd missed him. Missed. This. His fingers brushed across her clit, and she nearly came off the bed, gasping at the sparks that flew through her.

"Ah, you're wet." Satisfaction rumbled in his voice. "I should taste."

"Not yet." She dug her hands into his shoulders, feeling the muscles bunch beneath her palms. "Later. Now. Just you and me." More than anything in the world, she needed him inside her again. It had been five years. Five lonely, sad, empty years.

His gaze softened. "You have to be ready." The smile curving his lips was all rogue as he swept his fingers across her clitoris again. "I think I remember how to get you there." He kissed her deep, his fingers working their magic.

She gasped and pressed against him, her mouth overtaken and her body alighting. He inserted one finger inside her and pressed his thumb against her clit. It was almost embarrassing how quickly she orgasmed. She tensed and came down with a soft moan. More. She definitely needed more of him.

He nipped her lip and let her breathe. "There you go." Then he pressed into her, going slow, the muscles bunching in his neck as he held himself back. Then he paused. "You still on the pill?"

She'd forgotten. Actually forgotten. "Yes, and I'm clean."

"Ditto." He pushed inside her again, sliding along nerves that nearly sent her over the edge.

She stretched to accommodate him, trying not to wince. Had he gotten even bigger? She wiggled against him, trying to hurry him up, but he took his time.

Finally, he was inside her, all of him. He smoothed the hair back from her face, his gaze both gentle and intense. Then he pulled out to push back inside her. Even deeper this time. She gasped and widened her thighs, shifting restlessly against him.

He thrust again, and she moaned. Then he set up a slow and relentless rhythm, still in control, keeping her on the edge and taking every bit of her with each thrust. His mouth wandered along her jaw and down her neck, moving up to bite her earlobe. "When I was over there, doing things I can't talk about, I thought of you. Of you in the sunshine, of you in the rain, and of you just like this," he whispered, his mouth hot on her skin.

She blinked. "I thought about you all the time."

His movements increased in force and speed, taking her over. She dug her fingers into his shoulders and then down his rigid arms, trying to wrap them around his wrists.

He pounded harder, and she lifted her hips to meet his thrusts, wanting never to let him go again. His teeth latched onto her shoulder, and she cried out. It was one more sensation piled on a million others, all centered around Hunter Holt. An orgasm swelled inside her, forcing her to climb, just out of her reach.

He reached between them and brushed his thumb across her clit.

Wild coils sparked inside her, and she shut her eyes as the room sheeted hot and white and blinding. A liquid rush of pure pleasure took her, and she whispered his name, her body gyrating as the climax stole her breath.

In the far distance of reality, she felt his arm wrap around her waist and pull her off the bed as he gave one last, hard shove inside her. His mouth found her neck, and he groaned, his body shaking with his climax.

She gasped, her heart thundering, as she came down. He lay on top of her, most of his weight held by his arms. She was spent, exhausted, and so satisfied she could purr like a kitten. He rolled them over, curling around her, his big body protecting her from any possible danger in this world.

Sex with Hunter had always been incredible. Wild and complete. But this had felt different. They were adults, both settled in life, and no promises had been made. He tightened his hold around her, and she settled against his hard body.

What did this mean? What did she want it to mean? Aside from everything. Hunter had always held a part of himself back, and she understood that. But she needed all of him for it to work. He'd promised her nothing, but even now, she knew without question he'd protect her with his life in a second. If danger came through the door, he'd be between her and the outside in a heartbeat.

But would he give her his heart? Completely?

He lived with so many ghosts already. What if they couldn't save Jackson? Would there be anything left of Hunter?

Chapter Twelve

Jackson Holt sat on a bed in a motel room somewhere in the middle of Montana. They'd driven all night from South Dakota to this small town, and he was tired of being on the road. Soon they'd be at the lake in Washington state where Louise had happy memories. She deserved happy memories, and he'd help her make some more.

She was out getting something to eat, and she'd left the shotgun as well as the handgun, so he could relax a little. They'd mainly slept in the car and at campgrounds, so it was nice being in a motel again.

He flicked on the television, but it didn't work. Louise had mentioned that when he'd been in the shower earlier. It had been about a week since he'd caught up on the world. Were he and Louise mentioned on the news as missing? Surely her robberies had been covered, although they'd crossed several states, so maybe not.

He pushed himself off the worn bedspread toward the box television on the rickety old table. Then he leaned down and looked at the back. It was unplugged. Awareness crackled over his skin. Louise would've figured that out, right? He bit his lip, plugged the cord in, and turned on the television.

A show on fishing in Montana came up first. He changed channels, caught a rerun of *The Office* and watched for a while. Then the news came on, flashing his picture as well as Louise's—

along with a report that a policeman she'd shot was recuperating in South Dakota.

She'd shot a cop?

What the hell? That was a capital offense. Even he knew that.

Oh, he had to find out more information. How could he access the internet?

He needed his phone, but they'd destroyed all electronics and left them behind in either Iowa or Illinois. The states were running together in his head. Shoving a ball cap on his head, he strode outside and ran across the dirt road to a lonely-looking casino. Only the sign's C and N were lit up. Once inside, the smoke hit him first, followed by the stench of mold. A couple of old guys played video poker in the corner, while most of the machines remained empty.

He meandered around a corner toward a small restaurant, where a family sat at a far booth. Damn it. The kids were too young to be of help.

A counter ran the length of the kitchen with blue stools, and a waitress of about twenty stood by the cash register, her blond hair streaked purple. He moved toward her, already plastering on his smoothest smile.

She straightened and smiled back. "Hi." Her gaze wandered down to his boots and back up, and that smile widened.

Yeah, for sixteen, he had decent muscle tone, and with his scruff, he looked older. Not nearly as tough or mean as that half-brother of his he'd just met, but he could deal with a bored waitress. He grinned. "Hi. I just wanted to buy a Pepsi to go." He handed over a hundred dollar bill.

She blinked. "I don't think I have that kind of change."

Neither did he. "It's okay. How about you give me the drink, and you put the rest in a machine? If you win, we split it."

Her eyes danced. "Deal." She quickly turned and poured a Pepsi out of the machine.

Ah. There was his chance. When she came around, he barely stuck his foot out. She tripped, and he caught her easily, helping her up.

"I'm such a klutz," she muttered, her face turning pink.

Yeah, but she was cute. It was too bad he'd learned to manipulate people early in his life. He slipped the phone he'd taken from the back pocket of her jeans into his own and then led her to a slot machine. "Okay. You start with this one. I have to go check in with my boss since I'm on the road, but I'll be back in about fifteen minutes." He drank down half the Pepsi and set it next to her, so she'd think he was coming back. "Don't win too much without me."

She smiled. "I won't."

He quickly exited, already scrolling through the internet on the phone, looking for anything about himself or Louise. His chest felt like somebody punched him when he found the first news story. She'd killed people. As in dead. Hurt hit him next. The woman had lied to him. They'd promised never to lie to each other. He reached the motel and leaned against the hard cement blocks outside, banging his head back. There was no way out of this. What should he do? God. It was too much. He read more. Three dead. She'd shot at least six people, and three were dead. And she'd kidnapped an old lady.

His stomach lurched, and he ran around the side of the building to puke his guts out. The soda burned on the way back up, and he aimed for some dead bushes.

He wiped his mouth and looked at the phone. Not knowing why, he video dialed the number that had called him the other day. He had a thing with numbers—only had to see them once and they stuck in his head. Not that his father ever took notice of the talent.

His face, or rather, an older and tougher version of his face, came up on the screen. "What?" Hunter said, his gaze narrowing as recognition came into his eyes. "Hey, Jackson. You okay?"

No, he wasn't okay. Not at all. "I didn't know," he whispered, his voice hoarse from the acid. "That she killed people. I didn't know." Nobody was going to believe that. Jesus, he was a moron.

"I believe you," Hunter said, his gaze intense. "I figured you had no idea. You weren't at any of the crime scenes."

Jackson wanted to cry. Even if the guy was lying, at least he said he believed him. Nobody ever had before. Well, except Louise, and now she'd lied to him. "I don't know what to do." He sounded young and desperate. His father was right. He was a weak loser. His shoulders hunched. Maybe the world was just better off without him.

"Tell me where you are, and I'll be there," Hunter said. "I'm headed your way now, and I can help you. You're only sixteen. You haven't committed a crime yet. We'll figure this out together."

There was nothing to figure out. Maybe if he'd known Hunter before, but it was too late. He'd been created by evil, and he was who he was. One person had shown him kindness, and he'd made a vow. She needed saving. "I love her." There wasn't a good ending here. No way to figure anything out. But maybe he could rescue her somehow and then take the fall. "I wish I could've known you, Hunter." Jackson clicked off.

Louise drove into the parking lot in an older white Chevy, her eyebrows drawn together.

Jackson met her at the car and threw the phone toward the bushes. "We need to get out of here. Now."

* * * *

Hunter drove through the night. A GPS trace had tracked the phone to a hotel in western Montana, so they stopped there briefly. A witness mentioned a white Chevy car. Hunter drove faster, following I-90 west while Raider worked on his phone and Faye tracked routes on the map toward the lake in Washington.

Raider's phone buzzed, and he answered. "Yeah. Okay. Got it." He hung up. "Traffic cams saw a Chevy like we're looking for in this area." He held up his phone to show a map of a small area in northern Idaho. It was a lake surrounded by private forest land. A lot of it. It'd be a great place to hide out if somebody knew how to live off the land. Maybe the fugitives had decided to stop there rather than continue on to Washington state. A private subdivision and lodge showed at the north end, surrounded by fences. Something similar lay to the west. Rich people did like their privacy.

Hunter studied the map. "We can take a look along that forest service road there. That can't be private." Sure, there would probably be fences, but he'd learned early on in life how to break a lock. His eyes were gritty and his gut uneasy. The tone in Jackson's voice hadn't been good. It was like the kid had given up once he learned the truth.

They drove for two more hours and finally reached the forested land. A search along a dirt road through thick pine trees ended with them finding the abandoned Chevy, along with other tire tracks. Shit. "They stole another car, drove them both here, and abandoned this one." Hunter stopped his SUV and jumped out, approaching the Chevy slowly. It was sheltered beneath two massive spruce trees and wouldn't have been visible if they hadn't followed the road.

It was empty of people. He gave a hand signal to Raider and Faye before setting his gun at the back of his waist. Then he opened the door.

Food wrappers, used deodorant, and magazines. Nothing of interest.

A stick snapped right before two men strode out of the forest. Broad-chested men, both at least six-foot-six and wearing insanely large combat boots and light-refracting glasses that hid the color of their eyes. The first guy had black hair to his shoulders with an odd gray strip on one side, while the other guy had long dark hair and an aura of pissed-off danger. His hair was pulled back and might have had a gray strip at the side partially covered. Definitely trained, and not happy to see people on the land.

Hunter pivoted, his instincts flaring. "Faye? Get back in the car."

Raider instantly moved his way, settling his shoulder against Hunter's, facing the threats.

Hunter surveyed the two. There was no doubt one of them had stepped on the stick on purpose. He knew that as well as he knew his own name. These guys could move without making a sound. He couldn't see a weapon on either one, but he wasn't certain they needed any.

"Hello," the guy with black hair said.

"You're trespassing," the other guy said, not bothering with the niceties.

Similar bone structure and same stubborn jaw. Brothers? Hunter nodded at the abandoned Chevy. "We're tracking my brother, who was taken by his teacher across state lines. I'm Hunter, and this is Raider."

"Dage," said the darker-haired guy, "and my brother, Talen." He tilted his head and focused on the SUV. "You are?"

"Faye Smith." Faye gingerly moved closer to Hunter, and he angled his body to keep her behind him. If the woman didn't see these guys as a threat, she needed some serious training in how to heed her instincts.

"It's nice to meet you," Dage said, his lips tipping in a smile.

Faye may have twittered. Seriously? Hunter widened his stance.

Talen lifted a phone from his back pocket. "North quadrant is secured. We have an abandoned vehicle. Check the plates." Leaning, he snapped a photo with his phone.

Two seconds later, a hoarse voice came through the speaker. "Stolen Chevy out of Butte, Montana. Owner is one Dixie Johnson."

Wow. Impressive contacts. Hunter tilted his head. "Any chance you saw the other vehicle that came through here?"

Talen typed into his phone and waited, then read the screen, flipping the page a couple of times. He slowly lowered the phone. "Red Ford truck, license plate "GoTeam." Stolen out of Wallace, Idaho, about four hours ago. Traffic cams show the driver as a young man aged fifteen to eighteen. Driver of the white Chevy a woman with dark hair, approximately age forty. Identified as Louise Stockley and Jackson Holt, wanted for several crimes, starting in Kentucky and ending in Idaho so far."

Jesus. Who were these guys?

Raider looked around at the innocuous trees. "Is this some sort of military facility?"

"No," Dage said smoothly. "Our middle brother is always inventing new surveillance equipment. Our cameras are often superior to others." He gave Talen a nod, who typed something else into his phone.

Talen read the screen and then looked up. "The red truck is in Washington state. Drove into a parking garage in Spokane about two hours ago. It'll take time to figure out what vehicle they stole there, if any."

All right. Those weren't simple cameras. Hunter cut Raider a look.

Dage smiled, all charm. "My brother might be able to hack into other cameras if the mood so strikes him. We don't like teachers kidnapping kids, either."

"Now it's time for you to go." Talen slipped his phone back into his pocket, his jaw rock hard. "We will send the information we have to the FBI, which is pursuing this case, according to my source. We'll also take care of this Chevy and make sure it is delivered to the authorities."

Dage smiled again. "Good luck finding your brother. As an eldest brother myself, I can understand the difficulty of keeping family safe."

Talen sighed, obviously the less friendly of the two. "Goodbye."

Well. That was a dismissal, and this time it was said with a rather threatening undertone. "Thanks for your help." Hunter returned to the vehicle and waited until Raider and Faye had shut their doors before slowly backing down the road.

"What the heck?" Faye asked, craning her neck for one last look at the brothers.

Hunter shrugged. "Heck if I know. But we were trespassing, so I guess it'll have to remain a mystery." Maybe the family was connected to the government or something. At this point, who knew?

He had bigger things to worry about.

Chapter Thirteen

Faye wore one of Hunter's engulfing shirts to bed while he and Raider talked in the other room, scouting different lakes in Washington and trying to figure out which one Jackson was headed toward. They'd gotten a suite in a nice hotel this time, one with two bedrooms. Would Hunter join her or crash on the sofa in the living area?

He'd been distant all day, but he'd been worried about Jackson. She could tell that meeting up with those two soldier-type guys in Idaho had thrown him a little, too. She got into bed, her head hurting, her chest tight.

When he came in an hour later, she was still awake.

She sat up. "You sleeping here?"

"Yeah." He ditched his clothes and slipped into bed, wearing only his boxer briefs. "We've narrowed down the area where they might be. Maybe?"

She rolled toward him, setting her cheek on her hand. "Do you regret last night?"

He exhaled, lying on his back, not looking at her. "No."

"But?"

He shook his head. "I can't think of us right now."

Yeah, but if things went badly when they found his brother, he'd never think of them. He'd drop into grief and guilt, and she'd never get him back. She hated forcing him to face feelings, but everything inside her told her it was now or never. When it came to him, her instincts were good, and she planned to heed them. "That's too bad, because we are going to think of us. Right here and right now."

"No." He rolled over, turning his back to her.

Oh. He. Did. Not.

She pulled the sheet up, then kicked him square in the ass as hard as she could. Pain ricocheted up her leg, but she didn't care.

He flipped over, facing her, staring at her like she'd gone crazy. His blue eyes glittered through the darkness, sparking as fury took him over. "What the hell did you just do?"

She shivered. Okay. That might've been stupid and over the line. She swallowed past a lump in her throat. "You turned your back on me, refusing to talk about what we need to discuss, so you deserved a kick in the butt." Man, her mouth would not stop. Why wouldn't her mouth stop talking?

He leaned up on his elbow, his very muscled arm in full view, his body bigger and stronger than hers could ever be. His mouth set in a hard line. For the first time, she could see the weapon he'd become for the military. "You've lost your mind," he rasped.

Yeah. More than likely. "I don't care. Talk to me, or I'll kick you again." Oh, she didn't just say that.

He moved then, flattening her on her back, his heated body over hers. A hot thrill shot through her, sparking each nerve. "If you ever kick me again, I promise you a regret you can't imagine right now."

She snorted. Actually snorted. Hunter Holt would cut off his right testicle before he'd harm a woman. "Whatever."

"You don't think I'd spank you?" Interest and something darker hinted in his rough tone.

Her mouth opened but no sound came out. A shiver wound down her body, landing right between her legs. Now that, she wasn't sure about. He seemed to think it was a fine idea. Her breath quickened, and not an ounce of it was from fear. Maybe anticipation. Okay. Perhaps a little fear. "Hunter."

"We're going to sleep now, Faye. Got it?"

She didn't want to sleep. Instead, she caressed her hand over his tattoo and down his back, admiring every single muscle. His shoulders, his back, and around his ribs to that six-pack of abs. Even the indents above his butt felt the rub of her fingers. "I don't want to sleep." She allowed vulnerability in, because it was the only way they could work. "I'm not letting you push me away again."

"You left," he reminded her, desire darkening his tone.

"We both did," she said softly. He'd retreated emotionally as surely as she had physically. But it didn't matter. Not anymore. All she had to give him, no matter what happened, was herself. He had to know that before the next day arrived, in case it was a bad one. It might be. She widened her thighs, letting him rest against her. He was hard and aroused. "I trust you, Hunter. Completely."

His head jerked just enough to show the impact she'd had. "Don't trust me."

"I do." She reached up and dug her hands through his hair. "I'm not asking for anything from you. Not a thing. But I trust you and I love you. No matter what you do or don't do. No matter what happens ever. You have me for as long as you want me." She'd learned her lesson when she left last time. It was so clear to her now. He'd never been given real trust. Neither of them had. Unconditional trust and love. Everyone wanted love. It was the trust they'd never been able to even ask for—from anybody.

He just looked at her, his gaze shielded, the tension in his muscles obvious against her. Resisting her. What she offered.

Protectiveness roared through her. A need to show him that he wasn't alone. That he'd never be alone again. That he was enough and everything wasn't his fault. "You're a good man, Hunter Holt."

The denial was there in his eyes, on his lips. So she kissed him before he could answer. "You survived childhood, and you did your job in the military. Despite anything you've done, anything you'll ever do, I accept you. I trust you and I love you." She laid herself bare, because he was worth it. He needed to know the truth—even if he left.

If she'd been in her right mind, she would've given him everything before. Now, with time and distance, she could see what he needed. What only she could give to him. Herself.

He fought it hard. She could see resistance on his face and feel the battle in his body. When he shuddered, when he lowered his forehead to hers, her chest hitched. She'd won. All of him. She could feel it.

"I love you," he said, his mouth against hers. "Completely and forever. I trust you, too."

The words slid through her, bringing tears that filled her soul. Finally. Trust.

She yanked off her shirt while he finished stripping them both. His kiss was frantic, his fingers against her core quick and perfect. "I'm ready now," she whispered against his mouth, meaning it. She was wet and needy. For him. "Please, Hunter. Inside me. Now." Only he could fill her.

He entered her, hard and fast, stealing her breath. Pain and pleasure collided, overtaking her. Then he was moving. Fast and hard and complete. All of him inside of her—the sensations so complete she could barely breathe. Then he stopped.

She grabbed his flanks, an orgasm so close. "What are you doing?" she gasped.

He looked down at her, so strong and male, so intense. Possessive and real. "This is forever. You and me. I'm not letting you go again."

"I know." She clapped her thighs against his hips. She'd known that fact the second he'd said he loved her.

"Good." Grabbing her hip, he powered inside of her, going deep and hard. An orgasm rolled over her, taking everything she had. She held on tight, knowing he'd keep her safe. No matter what.

He kissed her again, her name on his lips as he ground against her and came.

They both breathed heavily as he rolled them over and gathered her close. She shut her eyes, finally at home. No matter what the next day brought.

* * * *

Jackson Holt pulled the truck around the lake to the farthest campground, rolling to a stop beneath the boughs of an ancient pine tree. Maybe not ancient, but definitely old. Louise slept with her head against the window, her face smooth in the soft moonlight. This was what love felt like, right?

He'd lied to her earlier to get her to leave Montana quickly, telling her he saw a couple of police cars go by. She'd be angry if she knew he'd talked to his brother, and there was no reason to tell her.

His mind was made up. She'd risked everything to love him, and that had to be respected. A tiny niggle of doubt swept through his head. It wasn't the age difference, or the fact that she was married. Or even that she'd killed people. Oh, that was wrong, and he felt bad—sick, really—about it. But she had been hurt, badly, not just in her marriage, but as a kid by a man who shouldn't have touched her. She'd told Jackson all about it.

It was the fact that she'd lied to him after everything they'd told each other.

He'd told her about his father, who liked to hit. How he figured it was his fault. But she'd said it wasn't, and while he hadn't believed her, something had shifted inside him when he'd seen his brother. When Hunter Holt had said he believed Jackson.

Louise stirred and sat up, blinking. "Where are we?"

"Walimi Lake. A campground on the south side," he said, scouting the area for threats.

She turned and smiled, love in her eyes. "You let me sleep."

"I'm going to protect you," he said, lowering his chin. "No matter what. You get that, right?"

She blinked again. "Of course. We love each other." She stretched her neck and tugged her sweatshirt into place. "There's a convenience store on the other side of the lake. I'll go find us some food and money."

"No." He turned to study her. "You can't rob them. Not if we're planning to stay here."

She rubbed her eyes. "But we need money and food."

"I'll get a job, and I'll support you. No more robbing." He waited until she looked at him. "Or killing."

She exhaled. "How did you know?"

"Saw the television." He wanted to help her more than anything else in the entire world. "No more. Promise me."

She swallowed, and he could see the indecision in her eyes. Then she smiled. "All right. No more killing."

His gut sank. Hard and fast, like a fist he'd taken there more than once. He knew the signs of somebody lying. The shifty eyes, the wide smile, the soft voice. His father lied like that. As had several other people in his life. Louise was no different from the rest of them. And she killed, he realized, because she liked to kill. "I love you," he said, meaning it.

She patted his cheek. "I love you, too."

This wasn't love. It was the closest he'd ever been or would ever get, but it wasn't the real thing. The real thing didn't include lies or guns or shooting people for money. Shit, he'd never been so confused.

He'd do anything to talk to Hunter again. Just once. What would his life have been like if he'd met Hunter before he'd met Louise? Well. It didn't matter, now did it? "What do you want to do, Louise?" he asked quietly. "No lying or playing games. What's the plan?"

She eyed him and licked her lips, taking the shiny silver gun out of the glovebox. "I really want to hit the convenience store on the other side of the lake."

His chest hollowed out. Would she shoot him if he refused? The safety was off, and even though the gun rested on her leg, the barrel faced him. But he'd learned from the best, so he pursed his lips like he was thinking really hard. "Then we can't stay here." The dream of them building a life at this pretty lake disappeared faster than that money he'd made mowing lawns one summer. Ramsay had found it, even though he'd hidden it well.

"I know." She hopped on the seat, and the gun jumped. "But we'll find another place. A safe place for just us. Okay?"

His chin dropped, and his entire body felt like he was eighty years old. "Yeah. Okay."

Chapter Fourteen

The call came in during their third hour of scouring maps of different lakes in Washington state. A robbery and hostage situation at a convenience store at Walimi Lake. Hunter broke every speeding law on record to get there in time, his heart racing and his gut churning. They pulled up, right between two worn brown county patrol cars.

The store looked like a log cabin with a green metal roof. A wide porch extended around the front and the lake sparkled out back. Two newspaper dispensers stood by the door, which was shut with the blinds closed. Trees rose high all around them, but the birds had been silenced by the disturbance. In the distance, a boat roared across the water.

"Status?" Raider asked, jumping out of the SUV, flashing his HDD badge immediately.

A gnarled sheriff with shrewd blue eyes looked over from his car. "Got the call you'd be here. Inside are just the two fugitives right now. Louise Stockley and that kid, Jackson Holt."

Hunter straightened to look at the sheriff. "Hostages?"

"Let go," the sheriff confirmed. "Besides the owner, Al Burtley, there was a family of four who stopped by for supplies and two teenagers who were here for lattes. They all said the kid told them to go and scuffled with the woman so they could. They ran down the road and called us. We had them taken to the hospital, per procedure. Except for Al. He wouldn't leave."

Hunter's chest heated. "Was anybody hurt?"

"No," the sheriff said, his gray hair pulled back at the nape.

The backdoor to his car opened, and a grizzly man the size of a bear stood up. He had short white hair, a long white beard, and faded green eyes that matched his T-shirt. "I'm Al."

Hunter swung around the SUV with Faye on his tail. "What happened in there?"

Al shook his large head. "The kid had a handgun, and the woman a shotgun. She pointed it at me, and the kid shoved her into a wall, yelling for all of us to run. We did while he held her. Then, once we were out, somebody locked the door."

Shit. Hunter looked toward the quiet store. His brother had no intention of coming out. Not one. He looked down at Faye, not surprised by the sheen of tears in her eyes.

She sniffed. "I understand. Remember I love you." She hugged him tight, feeling small and vulnerable against him.

A lump centered in his throat as she released him.

Raider grabbed him for a hard hug. "I love you, brother."

Hunter nodded, holding his brother for a moment. He stepped back. "Take care of each other, if…"

They both nodded.

The sheriff grabbed his arm. "Wait a minute. You can't—"

Raider held up the badge again. "This is a federal matter, sheriff. Let him go." His voice was low and rough, the emotion in it obvious.

The sheriff released Hunter.

He turned and strode for the door, not looking back. He couldn't look back. His footsteps were heavy on the porch, and it took him a minute to realize Raider was at his side. He frowned. "Get the hell back," he whispered.

Raider looked him right in the eye, his eyes blacker than normal. "Brothers forever. It's that simple."

God, it really was. Hunter nodded, letting himself trust. "All right." Raider wouldn't hurt Jackson. Hunter knocked hard. "Jackson? It's Hunter."

"Go away, Hunter," Jackson called. "Get out of here."

He was alive. The kid was still alive. Relief threatened to drop Hunter until the adrenaline from the danger they all faced flashed through him. He swallowed. "Not gonna happen, kid. I'm coming in. That's what family does. Either unlock the door, or I'm kicking it down."

A shotgun cocked.

"No, Louise," Jackson yelled. "Don't."

"Now," Hunter said, kicking in the door. He went low and left, while Raider went high and right.

Louise fired, hitting the glass part of the door, spraying shards in every direction. One cut into Hunter's neck, but he kept going, searching for Jackson.

Jackson tackled Louise to the floor, and a gun discharged.

"No!" Hunter yelled, sliding across glass to reach his brother. He rolled Jackson over, and blood burst across the kid's chest. "Jackson. Hold on, buddy." Oh, God. Hunter panicked, looking for the wound.

Raider rushed by and flipped Louise over, pinning her hands behind her back. The sheriff ran inside and tossed him handcuffs, which he quickly slipped into place.

She struggled and cried as Raider yanked her to her feet.

Hunter frantically searched for the bullet hole. Jackson's entire chest was covered with blood.

Louise looked down, sobbing. "Jackson? My Jackson?"

"I'm not yours, you crazy hag," Jackson moaned, slapping at Hunter's hands. "Dude. Stop pushing on me."

Hunter ripped open the kid's shirt and slid his hands through the blood, finding the wound in the upper right shoulder. Thank God. Okay. He pressed against it to stem the blood.

Jackson winced. "Stop it. Geez. As a brother, you suck so far," he gasped.

Tears burned Hunter's eyes. "I'll get better. I promise." He looked over at Raider, who was bleeding from glass in his forehead.

Then Faye came inside and rushed over, dropping to her knees. She set her hand down and winced as glass cut into her palm. Her brown eyes were panicked and her blond hair mussed. She looked perfect. "Is he okay?" A siren sounded in the distance.

"He will be," Hunter said, keeping his hold firm. Okay. Almost everyone he loved in the world was in the room bleeding. But they were all gonna be okay. He'd make sure of it.

Epilogue

Faye sat on the sofa as Miss Angelina fussed around, making sure there was enough sweet tea and cookies. The elderly woman had dressed in her best mint green suit and hat today, and it was apparent she had an announcement to make. Or perhaps she was waiting for one. Either way, it was a nice spring day, and Faye was enjoying herself.

"You pick those classes yet?" Miss A asked.

Faye nodded happily. "Yep. Landscape design, and Mr. Moriarty said I could already start working with him while going to school." Moriarty's Landscaping was the best around. "He'd like to retire sometime, and since his kids both became lawyers, he's thrilled."

"Good." Miss A nodded, her eyes gleaming. It was like she'd had a plan all along.

Jackson sat in a chair by the fireplace, his arm in a cast and a puppy on his lap. He'd been released from the hospital the day before, back into Miss Angelina's custody, since she'd had him last. He'd been quiet most of the morning as they waited for Hunter to return, but his face had lost that pinched and worried look. And he was on his third cookie.

Hunter came in the front door and wiped off his boots, even though there probably wasn't anything on them. He wore dark jeans and a blue button-down shirt that made his eyes appear deep and mysterious. He filled it out like it had been made for him, making him look strong and sure.

Jackson tensed and sat up straighter, his face turning pale. "Did you get Raider off okay?"

Raider had to get back to that crazy deep ops group and go undercover, which Faye was not happy about. She'd figure out a way to get him safe once they had Jackson all settled in.

Hunter nodded. "I stopped by the courthouse as well."

Faye set down her tea. Her stomach turned over. "What did they say?"

Jackson looked down at his hands.

Hunter shut the door and waited for Miss Angelina to take a seat before he continued. "The prosecutor has reviewed all the evidence and has agreed to grant Jackson immunity if he testifies against Louise." Hunter looked at his younger brother. "The fact that you let those people go and then tried to save me worked strongly in your favor."

Jackson swallowed. "Testify against Louise?"

"You just have to tell the truth," Faye said, reaching over to pat his hand. The puppy licked her, and she smiled.

Jackson nodded.

Hunter studied him carefully. "I told them you'd agree. There's a good chance she'll plea, but you need to be prepared just in case." He gave a slight nod. Apparently he already knew that the woman would most likely plea. Good.

"So I stay here," Jackson said, stroking the puppy. "Okay."

"No." Hunter waited until the kid looked up. "I've petitioned for custody of you. Miss Angelina is an amazing woman, and she's our family. But I want you with me. For good."

Jackson froze. He swallowed several times, his gaze down. Were those tears? "All right."

Faye's eyes burned, and she blinked them away. No wonder she loved this guy.

Hunter nodded at Miss Angelina. "We've already talked to the mayor, and I'm set to replace the chief within the month. The guy doesn't know what he's doing, and it's time for me to do what I do best." He grinned. "Besides fish on the weekends, of course."

Of course. Faye nodded. It was good he was getting back into law enforcement.

Hunter cleared his throat and moved toward her. "And I want you with me, too." He dropped to one knee and whipped out a velvet box. "I asked Miss Angelina for her blessing, since she's basically the one who has always loved us. She said yes." He opened the box to reveal a stunning square diamond in white gold. "What do you say? I love you and I trust you forever." He grinned. "Forget all of those last names you've tried. How about you take mine? For good?"

She couldn't breathe. The diamond was beautiful, but forever was even better. Faye Holt. It had a seriously good sound to it. In fact, it was the name she'd been waiting her whole life to claim as her own. Just as Hunter had claimed her.

Jackson cleared his throat. "We'd be a family, Faye. Just think of it."

Aww. He was trying to convince her.

She lifted her face to Hunter's, her vision completely blurry from tears. "Yes."

Sneak Peek

Read on for an excerpt from Rebecca Zanetti's
next Deep Ops novel, FALLEN!

Coming soon!

CHAPTER 1

The smell of wood polish and lemons mixed with the smooth male scent of the way too respectable man sitting across the round table from Brigid. Everything about Raider Tanaka was clean cut, upstanding, and unyielding. Even his perfectly tailored navy blue suit with striped green power tie made him appear like a guy who daily helped old ladies cross the street. "You look like a Fed," she whispered.

His black eyes glimmered. "I am a Fed," he whispered back, his voice low and cultured.

Yeah, and that was a problem. She looked around the darkened Bostonian bar, where the attire of the patrons ranged from guys wearing worn dock clothes at the long bar to handmade silk suits over in the corner. Bodyguards with bulges beneath their jackets stood point near the guys with nice suits.

She shivered. "I don't think we blend in."

"I believe that's the point, Irish," Raider said, using a nickname he'd given her the first day they'd met. He finished off his club sandwich. His angular features showed his part-Japanese heritage, giving him an edgy look that contrasted intriguingly with his stock-broker-like suit. Just who was this man?

She shook her head. "I don't get it. Angus sent us here just to have lunch?" The plane ride alone from DC would've cost a mint, even though they'd sat in coach. Of course.

"The boss always has a plan," Raider said, tipping back his iced tea while eyeing the suits in the corner.

Aye, but it would be nice to know the plan. Brigid enjoyed working for the rag-tag Homeland Defense unit run by Angus Force, but her job was hacking computer systems or writing code. Certainly not having a weird lunch with her handler in Boston. "Should we be doing something?"

Raider shrugged and gestured toward her Cobb salad. "You going to finish that?"

"No." Her stomach was all wobbly.

"Okay." He slid his empty plate to the side and tugged hers toward him, digging in.

Her mouth gaped open. Straight-laced Raider Tanaka did not seem like the kind of guy to share somebody else's food. Not a chance. She'd figured him for some dorky germ-a-phobe, albeit a good looking one.

"What?" His dark eyebrows lifted. When she didn't answer, he glanced down at the lettuce. "When you grow up on the streets or in foster care, you take food where you can get it." Then he munched contentedly on a crouton.

She blinked, her mind spinning. "You grew up in foster care?" She'd have bet her last dollar, if she had one, that he'd grown up in Beverly Hills somewhere with a maid or two cleaning up his room and making his bed. His suits had to cost a fortune, and he had that prep-school look.

"Yes." Raider leaned back in his chair. "You're not the only one who's tough to figure out."

She tried to keep eye contact but found it difficult. Her abdomen warmed, and an interesting tingling licked along her skin. She had to do something about this disastrous attraction she had for him.

His gaze narrowed, while his back somehow straightened even more. That quickly, he went from lazily amused to alert and tense.

Her breathing quickened in response.

A man appeared by their table. One of the guys with the bulging jackets. "Can I help you?"

Raider looked up, a polite smile curving his lips. "Not unless you're serving dessert."

Brigid breathed in through her nose and exhaled slowly. Adrenaline flooded her system. "We're fine," she said.

The guy didn't look at her. His hair was slicked back, revealing beady brown eyes and a nose that had been flattened permanently to the left. A scar cut through the side of his bottom lip. "You look like a Fed."

Raider smiled, flashing even white teeth. "So I've heard."

"It's time for you to leave," the guy said, resting his hand on his belt.

"No," Raider said, his voice almost cheerful.

Brigid began to rise. "Raider, I think—"

"Sit down." Raider kept his gaze on the man with the gun, but the barked command in his voice had her butt hitting the seat in instant response.

She blinked. What the heck had just happened? "Um."

The armed man leaned in toward Raider. "I tear apart Feds for fun. Now get the pretty redhead out of here before I decide to rip off your head and show her what a real man can do with an hour or two."

Brigid's hands curled over the table, and she looked frantically around. The door was so close. She focused back on Raider.

If anything, he looked a little bored. "My money would be on the redhead," he said, losing his smile. "Now, friend. You can either go get us a dessert menu, or you can fuck off and slink back to your bodyguard duties."

Brigid swallowed a gasp. Had Raider just said the F-word? She glanced toward the corner, where one of the other bodyguards had started walking their way. This was about to get bad. She wasn't armed. Was Raider? He couldn't be. They'd flown commercially, and he hadn't declared a gun.

They had to get out of there. Right now.

The guy grabbed Raider by the tie, and then everything happened so quickly that Brigid didn't see all of it.

Raider stood in one easy motion, manacled the back of the guy's neck, and smashed his head so hard into the table that it cracked in two. Dishes and utensils flew in every direction while the guy and the wood crashed to the floor.

Brigid's chair rocked back, and she yelped, scrambling to her feet to keep from falling. The guy on the floor didn't move.

The easy and brutal violence coming from Raider shocked her more than the fight itself.

"Hey!" The other bodyguard, a red-headed man with a barrel of a chest, ran forward while yanking out his gun.

Raider pivoted and kicked the guy beneath the chin, sending him down and following like a blur of motion. Three punches and a quick twist, and Raider stood with the gun pointed at the back table. When he lifted his chin, the two men there lifted their hands.

The remaining patrons watched on, not moving.

Raider straightened his tie.

Brigid could only gape, her mind fuzzing. What had just happened? Raider backed toward her. "Door. Now."

She turned and stumbled for it just as sirens echoed down the street. Running outside into a light rain, she rushed for the passenger side of the compact they'd rented at the airport. Raider calmly entered the driver's seat, ignited the engine, and drove away from the restaurant.

Brigid gulped down panic, struggling to secure her seat belt. "I don't understand. Why in the hell were we sent to that restaurant?"

Raider set the confiscated gun between them and maneuvered around traffic. "I have a feeling our mission went according to plan." His hands were light on the steering wheel, but his voice held a tone she couldn't identify. She looked him over. He appeared like he'd been out for a relaxing lunch with a friend and hadn't probably just put two guys—two tough guys—in the hospital for a week.

Just who was Raider Tanaka?

After a silent plane ride back to DC, where Brigid ran over every moment of the day in her head and Raider read a series of HDD reports, they finally ended up at their headquarters just as night began to fall. As usual, the dilapidated elevator hitched at the bottom floor and then remained quiet.

"I hate this thing." Raider smacked his palm against the door. "Open, darn it."

The door hitched open.

Humor bubbled through the unease in Brigid. "You're magic."

He looked over his shoulder. "You have no idea, Irish." Then he crossed into the small and dimly lit vestibule of the basement offices.

Had he just flirted with her? For Pete's sake. She moved out of the claustrophobia inducing space on wobbly legs, the day just overwhelming on too many levels. Enough of that silliness. Reaching the wide-open room, she sighed. The fresh paint had brightened the office a bit, but the myriad of desks was still old and scarred, and the overhead lights old, yellow, and buzzing.

Raider looked down at the cracked concrete floor and shook his head.

"We're supposed to paint that next," Brigid said, coming up on his side. Wasn't that the plan? "And I think there's art coming, or screens that show outside scenes." The basement headquarters were a step down from depressing, even with the fresh paint. The big room was eerily silent, as well.

Three doors led to an office and two conference rooms, while one more door, a closet for the shrink, was over to the west.

A German shepherd padded out of the far office, munching contentedly on something bright red. It coated his mouth and stained the lighter fur around his chin.

"Roscoe," Brigid breathed, her entire body finally relaxing. Animals and computer code, she knew. It was people who threw her.

The dog seemed to grin and bounded toward her, his tail wagging wildly. She ducked to pet him. "What in the world do you have?" This close she could see that the stuff was thick and matted in his fur. She frowned and tried to force open his mouth. "Roscoe?"

As if on cue, Angus Force stepped out of the second conference room, also known as Case Room Two. "Hey, you two. How was Boston?"

Brigid looked up. "Roscoe has something."

"Damn it." Angus made it through the desks in record time. "Is it Jack Daniels?"

Brigid craned her neck to see. "No. It's red." The dog had a well-known drinking problem.

Angus glared at his dog. "Drop it. Now." The command in his voice would've made Brigid drop anything she was carrying.

The dog sighed and spit out a gold-plated lipstick.

Brigid winced. "That looks expensive."

The dog licked his lips.

Angus sighed. "I told everyone not to leave makeup around. He likes the taste."

"No, you didn't," Brigid countered.

Angus pierced her with a look. "Well, I meant to. Roscoe, get back to the office. Now."

The dog gave her a "what a butthead" type of look and turned to slink back to Angus's office.

"You two, come with me." Angus turned and headed back to the case room, no doubt expecting them to follow.

Raider motioned her ahead of him. Yeah. Like she'd return to that death trap of an elevator. Though it was preferable to dealing with Angus Force. The former FBI profiler now headed up this division of the HDD, and he seemed almost able to read people's minds. Was he reading hers? Did he have one clue that she wasn't who she was supposed to be? How much had he guessed? More importantly, why had he sent her to Boston?

She crossed into the case room to face a whiteboard across from a conference table. Several pictures of men, some in their early seventies and some had to be in their twenties, were taped evenly across the expanse. "New case?" she asked.

"Yes." Angus gestured for them to sit. "Did anybody recognize you in Boston?"

It took her a second to realize he was talking to her and not to Raider. "Me?"

"Yes," Angus said.

What the heck? "Why would anybody have recognized me?" she asked, her senses thrumming.

Raider eyed her and then Angus. "Nobody recognized her. My best suit, that you asked me to wear, did get some attention, however."

Angus nodded. "I've already read the report."

Curiosity took Brigid as she sat down, with Raider sitting next to her.

Angus moved around to the board. "New case kicked to us by the HDD. They think it's crap, and I think it has merit. Either that, or somebody is messing with us."

Raider stiffened just enough that Brigid could feel his tension. "How so?"

"While the Irish mob no longer exists in Boston, there are criminals, past associates of the mob that have risen in the ranks and become threats recently," Angus said, standing big and broad on the other side of the table.

Brigid perched in her seat, still not seeing the connection. She had no problem hacking into criminal affairs, so perhaps that's why she was included on this op?

"How so?" Raider asked, all business.

"Instead of working within the usual, or rather former, hierarchy of the mob, these guys are outsourcing work to incredibly skilled computer criminals," Angus said.

"Like me," Brigid said quietly.

Angus nodded. "Exactly. We have a line on a group using a site on the dark web. We think they're running drugs, but we don't know what else."

The dark web was nearly impossible to hack. "I can't just find a site without knowing where it is," Brigid said. "The key to bringing down somebody on the dark web is—"

"Getting them to meet you in person," Raider said. "Guess that's my part of this op."

"Partially," Angus said, eying them both. "There's more."

Warning ticked through Brigid. Why, she didn't know. But her instincts rose instantly, and she stiffened. "What?"

"We think this might be one of the key players." Angus turned and taped one more picture to the board.

Brigid stopped breathing. She stared at the picture. He had aged. His skin was leathery, his nose broken more than once, and his hair now all gray.

Raider glanced at her. "Who is that?"

"My father," she whispered. The man she hadn't seen or talked to in a long time. She coughed. "You're crazy. He's a farmer. Always has been."

Angus winced. "No. He was involved with the Irish mob for years. Formative ones. Then he supposedly got out, but now we think he's back in."

That couldn't be true. No way. "That's why you sent us to Boston? Those guys in the corner were mobsters?" Brigid gasped.

"Yep. Just wanted to see if you'd be recognized," Angus said.

"Damn it," Raider muttered. "You could've given me a heads up."

Brigid tried to rein in her temper. "Of course nobody recognized me. You're wrong about my father."

"Prove it," Angus said mildly. "You and Raider go talk to him and prove I'm wrong. But be prepared to be incorrect about this."

Brigid shook her head. "You want me to take an obvious government agent to my father's farm and what? Just ask him if he's involved in cybercrime?" No way. "Believe me. My dad wouldn't talk to a Fed if he was dying."

Angus's smile didn't provide reassurance. "No. You're going home to reconcile with your father because you've finally found your way in life with the man next to you—one with possible criminal ties that we're still working out. Who you want to introduce to your father before you marry."

"Marry?" Brigid blurted, her mind spinning wildly. "Are you nuts?" She turned to the straitlaced hottie next to her. "Tell him this won't work."

Raider hadn't moved. "This is important, Force?"

"Crucial," Angus affirmed. "There's more going on here than drugs. I just know it."

Raider turned and studied her with those deep and way too dark eyes. "Well, Irish. Looks like we're engaged." His smile sent butterflies winging through her abdomen. "This is going to be interesting. Now that you're mine, I will finally figure you out."

Please read on for an excerpt from Rebecca Zanetti's exciting Dark Protectors novel, VAMPIRE'S FAITH, available now!

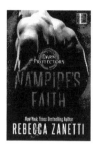

The Dark Protectors are Back!

Vampire King Ronan Kayrs wasn't supposed to survive the savage sacrifice he willingly endured to rid the world of the ultimate evil. He wasn't supposed to emerge in this time and place, and he sure as hell wasn't supposed to finally touch the woman who's haunted his dreams for centuries. Yet here he is, in an era where vampires are hidden, the enemy has grown stronger, and his mate has no idea of the power she holds.

Dr. Faith Cooper is flummoxed by irrefutable proof that not only do vampires exist . . . they're hot blooded, able to walk in sunlight, and shockingly sexy. Faith has always depended on science, but the restlessness she feels around this predatory male defies reason. Especially when it grows into a hunger only he can satisfy—that is if they can survive the evil hunting them both.

CHAPTER ONE

Dr. Faith Cooper scanned through the medical chart on her tablet while keeping a brisk pace in her dark boots through the hospital hallway, trying to ignore the chill in the air. "The brain scan was normal. What about the respiratory pattern?" she asked, reading the next page.

"Normal. We can't find any neurological damage," Dr. Barclay said, matching his long-legged stride easily to hers. His brown hair was swept back from an angled face with intelligent blue eyes. "The patient is in a coma with no brain activity, but his body is…well…"

"Perfectly healthy," Faith said, scanning the nurse's notes, wondering if Barclay was single. "The lumbar puncture was normal, and there's no evidence of a stroke."

"No. The patient presents as healthy except for the coma. It's an anomaly," Barclay replied, his voice rising.

Interesting. "Any history of drugs?" Sometimes drugs could cause a coma.

"No," Barclay said. "No evidence that we've found."

Lights flickered along the corridor as she passed through the doorway to the intensive-care unit. "What's wrong with the lights?" Faith asked, her attention jerking from the medical notes.

"It's been happening on and off for the last two days. The maintenance department is working on it, as well as on the temperature fluctuations." Barclay swept his hand out. No ring. Might not be married. "This morning we moved all the other patients to the new ICU in the western addition that was completed last week."

That explained the vacant hall and nearly deserted nurses' station. Only one woman monitored the screens spread across the desk. She nodded as Faith and Dr. Barclay passed by, her gaze lingering on the cute man.

The cold was getting worse. It was early April, raining and a little chilly. Not freezing.

Faith shivered. "Why wasn't this patient moved with the others?"

"Your instructions were to leave him exactly in place until you arrived," Barclay said, his face so cleanly shaven he looked like a cologne model. "We'll relocate him after your examination."

Goose bumps rose on her arms. She breathed out, and her breath misted in the air. This was weird. It'd never happened in the hospital across town where she worked. Her hospital was on the other side of Denver, but her expertise with coma patients was often requested across the world. She glanced back down at the tablet. "Where's his Glasgow Coma Scale score?"

"He's at a three," Barclay said grimly.

A three? That was the worst score for a coma patient. Basically, no brain function.

Barclay stopped her. "Dr. Cooper. I just want to say thank you for coming right away." He smiled and twin dimples appeared. The nurses probably loved this guy. "I heard about the little girl in Seattle. You haven't slept in—what? Thirty hours?"

It felt like it. She'd put on a clean shirt, but it was already wrinkled beneath her white lab coat. Faith patted his arm, finding very nice muscle tone. When was the last time she'd been on a date? "I'm fine. The important part is that the girl woke up." It had taken Faith seven hours of doing what she shouldn't be able to do: Communicate somehow with coma patients. This one she'd been able to save, and now a six-year-old girl was eating ice cream with her family in the hospital. Soon she'd go home. "Thank you for calling me."

He nodded, and she noticed his chin had a small divot—Cary Grant style. "Of course. You're legendary. Some say you're magic."

Faith forced a laugh. "Magic. That's funny." Straightening her shoulders, she walked into the ICU and stopped moving, forgetting all about the chart and the doctor's dimples. "What in the world?" she murmured.

Only one standard bed remained in the sprawling room. A massive man overwhelmed it, his shoulders too wide to fit on the mattress. He was at least six-foot-six, his bare feet hanging off the end of the bed. The blankets had been pushed to his waist to make room for the myriad of electrodes set across his broad and muscular chest. Very muscular. "Why is his gown open?"

"It shouldn't be," Barclay said, looking around. "I'll ask the nurse after you do a quick examination. I don't mind admitting that I'm stymied here."

A man who could ask for help. Yep. Barclay was checking all the boxes. "Is this the correct patient?" Faith studied his healthy coloring and phenomenal physique. "There's no way this man has been in a coma for longer than a couple of days."

Barclay came to a halt, his gaze narrowing. He slid a shaking hand through his thick hair. "I understand, but according to the fire marshal, this patient was buried under piles of rocks and cement from the tunnel cave-in below the Third Street bridge that happened nearly seven years ago."

Faith moved closer to the patient, noting the thick dark hair that swept back from a chiseled face. A warrior's face. She blinked. Where the hell had that thought come from? "That's impossible." She straightened. "Anybody caught in that collapse would've died instantly, or shortly thereafter. He's not even bruised."

"What if he was frozen?" Barclay asked, balancing on sneakers.

Faith checked over the still-healthy tone of the patient's skin. "Not a chance." She reached for his wrist to check his pulse.

Electricity zipped up her arm and she coughed. What the heck was *that*? His skin was warm and supple, the strength beneath it obvious. She turned her wrist so her watch face was visible and then started counting. Curiosity swept her as she counted the beats. "When was he brought in?" She'd been called just three hours ago to consult on the case and hadn't had a chance to review the complete file.

"A week ago," Barclay said, relaxing by the door.

Amusement hit Faith full force. Thank goodness. For a moment, with the flickering lights, freezing air, and static electricity, she'd almost traveled to an imaginary and fanciful place. She smiled and released the man's wrist. "All right. Somebody is messing with me." She'd just been named the head of neurology at Northwest Boulder Hospital. Her colleagues must have gone to a lot of trouble—tons, really—to pull this prank. "Did Simons put you up to this?"

Barclay blinked, truly looking bewildered. He was cute. Very much so. Just the type who'd appeal to Faith's best friend, Louise. And he had an excellent reputation. Was this Louise's new beau? "Honestly, Dr. Cooper. This is no joke." He motioned toward the monitor screen that displayed the patient's heart rate, breathing, blood pressure, and intracranial pressure.

It had to be. Faith looked closer at the bandage covering the guy's head and the ICP monitor that was probably just taped beneath the bandage. "I always pay back jokes, Dr. Barclay." It was fair to give warning.

Barclay shook his head. "No joke. After a week of tests, we should see something here that explains his condition, but we have nothing. If he was injured somehow in the caved-in area, there'd be evidence of such. But… nothing." Barclay sighed. "That's why we requested your help."

None of this made any sense. The only logical conclusion was that this was a joke. She leaned over the patient to check the head bandage and look under it.

The screen blipped.

She paused.

Barclay gasped and moved a little closer to her. "What was that?"

Man, this was quite the ruse. She was so going to repay Simons for this. Dr. Louise Simons was always finding the perfect jokes, and it was time for some payback. Playing along, Faith leaned over the patient again.

BLEEP

This close, her fingers tingled with the need to touch the hard angles of this guy's face. Was he some sort of model? Bodybuilder? His muscles were sleek and smooth—natural like a wild animal's. So probably not a bodybuilder. There was something just so male about him that he made Barclay fade into the *meh* zone. Her friends had chosen well. This guy was sexy on a sexy stick of pure melted sexiness. "I'm going to kill Simons," she murmured, not sure if she meant it. As jokes went, this was impressive. This guy wasn't a patient and he wasn't in a coma. So she indulged herself and smoothed his hair back from his wide forehead.

BLEEP

BLEEP

BLEEP

His skin was warm, although the room was freezing. "This is amazing," she whispered, truly touched. The planning that had to have gone into it. "How long did this take to set up?"

Barclay coughed, no longer appearing quite so perfect or masculine compared to the patient. "Stroke him again."

Well, all righty then. Who wouldn't want to caress a guy like this? Going with the prank, Faith flattened her hand in the middle of the guy's thorax, feeling a very strong heartbeat. "You can stop acting now," she murmured, leaning toward his face. "You've done a terrific job." Would it be totally inappropriate to ask him out for a drink after he stopped pretending to be unconscious? He wasn't really a patient, and man, he was something. Sinewed strength and incredibly long lines. "How about we get you out of here?" Her mouth was just over his.

His eyelids flipped open.

Barclay yelped and windmilled back, hitting an orange guest chair and landing on his butt on the floor.

The patient grabbed Faith's arm in an iron-strong grip. "Faith."

She blinked and then warmth slid through her. "Yeah. That's me." Man, he was hot. All right. The coming out of a coma and saying her name was kind of cool. But it was time to get to the truth. "Who are you?"

He shook his head. "*Gde, chert voz'mi, ya?*"

She blinked. Wow. A Russian model? His eyes were a metallic aqua. Was he wearing contacts? "Okay, buddy. Enough with the joke." She gently tried to pull loose, but he held her in place, his hand large enough to encircle her entire bicep.

He blinked, his eyes somehow hardening. They started to glow an electric blue, sans the green. "Where am I?" His voice was low and gritty. Hoarse to a point that it rasped through the room, winding around them.

The colored contacts were seriously high-tech.

"You speak Russian and English. Extraordinary." She twisted her wrist toward her chest, breaking free. The guy was probably paid by the hour. "The jig is up, handsome." Whatever his rate, he'd earned every dime. "Tell Simons to come out from wherever she's hiding." Faith might have to clap for her best friend. This deserved applause.

The guy ripped the fake bandage off his head and then yanked the EKG wires away from his chest. He shoved himself to a seated position. The bed groaned in protest. "Where am I?" He partially turned his head to stare at the now-silent monitor. "What the hell is that?" His voice still sounded rough and sexy.

Just how far was he going to take this? "The joke is over." Faith glanced at Barclay on the floor, who was staring at the patient with wide eyes. "You're quite the actor, Dr. Barclay." She smiled.

Barclay grabbed a chair and hauled himself to his feet, the muscles in his forearms tightening. "Wh—what's happening?"

Faith snorted and moved past him, looking down the now-darkened hallway. Dim yellow emergency lights ignited along the ceiling. "They've cut the lights." Delight filled her. She lifted her voice. "Simons? Payback is a bitch, but this is amazing. Much better than April fool's." After Faith had filled Louise's car with balloons filled with sparkly confetti—guaranteed to blow if a door opened and changed the pressure in the vehicle—Simons had sworn vengeance.

"Louise?" Faith called again. Nothing. Just silence. Faith sighed. "You win. I bow to your pranking abilities."

Ice started to form on the wall across the doorway. "How are you doing that?" Faith murmured, truly impressed.

A growl came from behind her, and she jumped, turning back to the man on the bed.

He'd just *growled*?

She swallowed and studied him. What the heck? The saline bag appeared genuine. Moving quickly, she reached his arm. "They are actually pumping saline into your blood?" Okay. The joke had officially gone too far.

Something that looked like pain flashed in his eyes. "Who died? I felt their deaths, but who?"

She shook her head. "Come on. Enough." He was an excellent actor. She could almost feel his agony.

The man looked at her, his chin lowering. Sitting on the bed, he was as tall as she was, even though she was standing in her favorite two-inch heeled boots. Heat poured off him, along with a tension she couldn't ignore.

She shivered again, and this time it wasn't from the cold.

Keeping her gaze, he tore out the IV.

Blood dribbled from his vein. She swallowed and fought the need to step back. "All right. Too far, Simons," she snapped. "*Waaaay* too far."

Barclay edged toward the door. "I don't understand what's happening."

Faith shook her head. "Occam's razor, Dr. Barclay." Either the laws of physics had just changed or this was a joke. The simplest explanation was that Simons had just won the jokester title for all time. "Enough of this, though. Who are you?" she asked the actor.

He slowly turned his head to study Dr. Barclay before focusing back on her. "When did the shield fall?"

The shield? He seemed so serious. Eerily so. Would Simons hire a crazy guy? No. Faith tapped her foot and heat rose to her face, her temper stirring. "Listen. This has been fantastic, but it's getting old. I'm done."

The guy grabbed her arm, his grip unbreakable this time. "Did both shields fail?"

Okay. Her heart started to beat faster. Awareness pricked along her skin. "Let go of me."

"No." The guy pushed from the bed and shrugged out of his gown, keeping hold of her. "What the fuck?" He looked at the Foley catheter inserted into his penis and then down to the long white anti-embolism stockings that were supposed to prevent blood clots.

Faith's breath caught. Holy shit. The catheter and TED hose were genuine. And his penis was huge. She looked up at his face. The TED hose might add a realistic detail to a joke, but no way would any responsible medical personnel insert a catheter for a gag. Simons wouldn't have done that. "What's happening?" Faith tried to yank her arm free, but he held her tight.

Dr. Barclay looked from her to the mostly naked male. "Who are you?" he whispered.

"My name is Ronan," the guy said, reaching for the catheter, which was attached to a urine-collection bag at the end of the bed. "What fresh torture is this?"

"Um," Faith started.

His nostrils flared. "Why would you collect my piss?"

Huh? "We're not," she protested. "You were in a coma. That's just a catheter."

He gripped the end of the tube, his gaze fierce.

"No—" Faith protested just as he pulled it out, grunting and then snarling in what had to be intense pain.

God. Was he on PCP or something? She frantically looked toward Barclay and mouthed the words *security* and *Get the nurse out of here.*

Barclay nodded and turned, running into the hallway.

"Where are we?" Ronan asked, drawing her toward him.

She put out a hand to protest, smashing her palm into his ripped abdomen. "Please. Let me go." She really didn't want to kick him in his already reddening penis. "You could've just damaged your urethra badly."

He started dragging her toward the door, his strength beyond superior. A sprawling tattoo covered his entire back. It looked like…a dark image of his ribs with lighter spaces between? Man, he was huge. "We must go."

Oh, there was no *we.* Whatever was happening right now wasn't good, and she had to get some space to figure this out. "I don't want to hurt you," she said, fighting his hold.

He snorted.

She drew in air and kicked him in the back of the leg, twisting her arm to gain freedom.

Faster than she could imagine, he pivoted, moving right into her. Heat and muscle and strength. He more than towered over her, fierce even though he was naked. She yelped and backpedaled, striking up for his nose.

He blocked her punch with his free hand and growled again, fangs sliding down from his incisors.

She stopped moving and her brain fuzzed. *Fangs?* Okay. This wasn't a joke. Somebody was seriously messing with her, and maybe they wanted her hurt. She couldn't explain the eyes and the fangs, so this had to be bad. This guy was obviously capable of inflicting some real damage. His eyes morphed again to the electric blue, and somehow he broadened even more, looking more animalistic than human.

"I don't understand," she said, her voice shaking as her mind tried to make sense of what her eyes were seeing. "Who are you? Why were you unconscious in a coma? How did you know my name?"

He breathed out, his broad chest moving with the effort. The fangs slowly slid back up, and his eyes returned to the sizzling aqua. "My name is Ronan Kayrs, and I was unconscious because the shield fell." He eyed her, tugging her even closer. "I know your name because I spent four hundred years seeing your face and feeling your soft touch in my dreams."

"My—my face?" she stuttered.

His jaw hardened even more. "And that was *before* I'd accepted my death."

CHAPTER TWO

Ronan kept a tight grip on the woman while moving out of the room into another area: A corridor of sorts with no windows. Why were there no windows? Was he underground? Only dim yellow candles glowed from the ceiling. "Where are we?" he asked, choosing a direction at random and moving.

She pulled back, digging in her heels.

He paused, not wanting to harm her. "Stop fighting me." They had to get away from this place with smells that burned his nostrils. What was that stench? Why had his cock, head, and arm been hooked up to those objects? "We must go." To have her in his hands after he'd given up the dream of her was too much. He needed to acquire safety and regroup. To find his people. Perhaps she could help him do so. "You're one of the Enhanced. Take me to your king."

She jerked her arm, nearly freeing herself. "King? Are you nuts?"

He blinked, looking down at her. She was smaller than she'd seemed in his dreams when she had whispered her name to him. Long black hair, olive-colored skin, stunning amber-colored eyes. Brown with a glow much brighter than in his dreams. She wore dark boots, blueish pants, a pink shirt with a white overcoat. "Nuts? No." Perhaps her king was dead. "Your father, then. Let's seek him."

Her chin lowered while her dark eyebrows rose. "Seek? All right, crazy man. Release me, now."

Why wasn't she cooperating? He stood to his full height. "I am Ronan Kayrs of the Kayrs ruling family. Obey me, woman."

She snorted.

He gaped. What had happened to the world he'd protected? A chill swept down his back, and he looked around. The floor was comprised of odd tiles, and boxes with blinking colors covered a raised table-like area. His heart thumped. "When am I?"

She kept her gaze on his face. "Excuse me?"

"Year, woman. Give me the year." He'd learned the hard way that time was fluid and felt different in other places. Other realms. "Or just a century. Give me that."

"Twenty-first century," she said, her voice softening along with her eyes. "Please let me get you some help. You're hurt."

He looked down at his mostly naked body. The holes in his head, arm, and inside his cock had already healed, but his knees still trembled. He wasn't at half-strength yet. And the long white material on his legs appeared ridiculous. "Are these the fashion of the day?"

She patted his arm, leaning toward him. "No. Those are to prevent blood clots, since you were lying in a bed."

Blood clots? "My blood doesn't clot." He bent, shoved the offending garments off with his free hand, and kicked them aside. He looked around. "I require clothing."

The tall man from earlier ran around a corner with two other men, these wearing brown garb with what appeared to be weapons at their belts. As soon as they came into sight, the first man drew back and let the other two with weapons slowly approach him.

"Don't hurt him," Faith said, holding out her hand to partially ward them off. "He's sustained extensive head trauma."

Truth be told, his head did hurt like a motherfucker. "Leave us," he ordered, not surprised when they continued advancing. "What the hell has happened to the world?" he muttered.

"Amen, buddy," Faith said, her body tensing. "Release me, and let's figure this out."

He looked around, his gaze catching on a drawing of himself lying on the table. "Did you draw that?"

She frowned and followed his gaze. "That's a picture of you. They probably put it on the news to see if you have any family or friends."

"The news?" His mind worked rapidly to catch up despite the headache. "That drawing was taken away and shown to others? Publicly?" How big was the world now? "When?"

"I don't know when," she said, pulling against his hold once more.

Pain flashed through his palm, burning up his arm and right into his heart.

She gasped and tried to jump back.

"Sorry," he said, wincing. It wasn't much of a surprise, though. "Did I burn you?"

Her eyes wide, she slowly nodded, her scent of wildflowers filling his head. "How did you...ah, do that?" Her hand was still up toward the advancing soldiers as if she was trying to keep control of the situation.

"It's the marking," he explained, facing her but tracking the men out of the corner of his eye. "The mating marking." How could she not be aware of the phenomenon?

"Huh?" she asked, her body tensing again.

What was happening? The two soldiers were getting closer, so he released her and held up his palm to show them the design. "Here. I am Ronan Kayrs. This is my marking, and this is my mate. I don't know to whom you align, but please take your leave."

The duo stopped.

Faith slowly backed toward the tall table. "Head injury," she said to the soldiers as if by way of explanation. "We need to get him to a room in the north wing." Then she studied his hand. "Nice tattoo."

Tattoo? "No. Marking." He looked at the jagged edges of his family marking with the K surrounded by fierce lines. "It appears when we find our mate. Surely you've dreamed of me."

"Right." She edged farther down the counter, her voice a little too high. "We're going to get you some help. I promise."

He turned his attention to the soldiers, seeking their vibrations. "You're human," he said, glancing instantly to his woman. "Why are human soldiers guarding you?" None of this was making sense, and it was time to go. "Faith?"

"Listen, buddy," the taller of the two men said, his gaze remaining on Ronan's face. "My name is Joe. I'm security, and I've been hit in the skull before. I know how you're feeling. How about we take you to the north wing so you can meet with a nice head doctor there and get some clothes?"

Ronan tilted his head to the side to study Joe. The man appeared to be about thirty years old with blond hair and earnest blue eyes. He looked fit and his hand rested lightly on a square-shaped contraption. "I do not wish to harm you, Joe." Even though Ronan was weak from the fall, he could overpower a couple of humans. Ronan checked out the other man. This guy was at least fifty, with a neatly trimmed gray beard and bushy hair. "Nor you, elder."

"Elder?" the guy asked, looking toward his friend. "All right." He drew a barrel-shaped weapon from his belt and pointed it at Ronan. "Enough talk."

"Agreed," Ronan said. Apparently, the soldiers weren't going to listen. He hated fighting naked. Nor would he attack two humans without further provocation.

"Joe?" the elder said.

"No—" Faith protested, just as Joe pushed something on the box.

Two wires sprang out, landing on Ronan's chest. Lightning shot through him, zipping painfully. He gasped, looking down at the twin metal squares. His innards protested, but he couldn't help but smile. Delight mixed with the pain. "You've learned to harness lightning." He yanked the offending wires out of his body and tossed them back at Joe. "Very impressive." He nodded at Faith. "Lightning. I never would've thought it."

Her chin dropped. "How are you still standing?"

Oh. "The weapon is probably meant for humans, sweetheart." His heart rate was slightly elevated, but it still clutched as a horrible thought hit him. "Tell me my people still exist." Of course they did. What a ridiculous fear. Vampires and demons couldn't be banished, even though he'd felt two of his brothers die. He just didn't know which two. Yet.

"Ah," she said, looking toward the soldiers. "Was that thing charged?"

"Yes," the elder said, moving to the left and pointing the other weapon at Ronan. "I don't want to shoot you, but I will."

Ronan sighed. "I do not particularly wish to be shot." The lightning had hurt and no doubt this was a bigger weapon. If they kept attacking him, he would never regain his strength. "What does that release?" Might it be fire? That could harm a vampire-demon hybrid.

"What's he on?" Joe asked Faith, looking down at his box.

"Undetermined," Faith said, squinting to study Ronan. "The tox report came back clear, but obviously…"

The air changed. The hair rose on the back of Ronan's neck. He inhaled, searching for a scent. "Faith. We must go." The drawings of him had called attention to his location. "Now." He moved toward her.

The elder fired.

Something exploded and pain ripped into Ronan's shoulder. Instinct took over, and he leaped across the space, grabbing the elder by the neck and throwing him into the wall. Before Joe could move, Ronan punched him squarely in the jaw, tossing him back several yards to land on the floor, where his head hit with a loud thump. The elder dropped to the ground, also unconscious.

Ronan rushed and grabbed the weapon from Joe before reaching for Faith. "I did not want to hurt them." But at least they'd live.

She cringed away, her gaze on the blood pouring from his shoulder. "You've been shot. Please let me take you to the surgical wing." Her fear was palpable, and the animal he kept bound deep inside began to stir in protest.

He looked down at the hole in his flesh. A metal of some type was embedded inside him, and he mentally shoved it out—but nothing happened. He was too weak. He tried to send healing cells to his wound, but it didn't close. Damn it. He required sustenance to rebuild himself.

Faith tried to back away.

"We have to leave," Ronan said, grasping her arm again. "Where is the exit to this place?" He looked around, seeing large doors at the opposite end of the hall. Perfect. The guards had arrived from the other direction. "Please don't fight me." His temper was finally starting to boil, and he needed time and space to figure out this new world. So, he started moving.

Faith hit him in the other arm and struggled, but he didn't stop this time. He'd have to explain everything to her once they were out of danger. It was coming closer and his breath quickened.

Those doors opened.

"What the hell?" Faith breathed, focusing on the enemy.

Ronan's chest settled. The metal object fell out of his shoulder, and his wound began to heal. He'd been too slow to get her to safety. "Apparently, your picture of me reached faraway villages."

"What in the world is he supposed to be?" she asked, her voice trembling.

"He is one of the Cyst," Ronan said, grateful she hadn't encountered them before. So, it wasn't known she was his mate. Good. Stretching his hands, he allowed weak power to clash through him. "Have you ever teleported?"

"Jesus," she muttered, shaking her head. "You're freaking crazy."

He drew on the elements of time and dimension, trying to make the jump.

Nothing.

"My powers haven't returned yet." Not a surprise, since he'd apparently been unconscious for quite some time. Well, he would have to fight, full power or not. It had been too long. "Stand out of the way, woman." He released her.

"Gladly." She turned in the other direction just as another Cyst soldier emerged through the doorway, standing guard on the other side of the downed human soldiers. "What the fuck?"

His woman had a mouth on her. Had she been shown no discipline in her life? That was about to change.

The first soldier moved forward, studying him. Apparently they had updated their uniforms through the years, from long black robes to black pants and shirts with matching boots. Their skin was a pasty white, their teeth yellow, and their eyes a blood purple. Only one strip of white hair ran down the middle of their heads, braided down their backs. Most Kurjans had red hair with black tips or black hair with red tips, but the Cyst, the special ones—they had white hair. Freaks.

Ronan growled.

The soldier moved closer, withdrawing a sword. "It is you. The Butcher."

Finally. A weapon Ronan recognized. Since they'd only sent two soldiers, it just must be a scouting party. Good. His hands itched with the need to do violence, although his body wanted to shut down. "I'd hoped the Kurjans had died out," he said, tensing his back leg.

"You tried." The Kurjan hissed and charged, swinging the sword in an arc. Ronan pivoted away from Faith and ducked. Then he turned quickly and kicked the Kurjan in the chest. The soldier fell back and then rushed forward again, his movements graceful but not nearly fast enough. He sliced down and Ronan dodged, striking the Kurjan's neck with the blade of his hand.

Bones shattered.

The Kurjan shrieked and fell back.

Ronan kicked him in the gut, spun, and claimed the sword. This male was barely trained. So, they hadn't trusted that picture and hadn't believed it was him. Or they would've sent a force. Thank the gods they hadn't. The Kurjan grabbed his neck, his eyes morphing to a pure red.

Ronan swung and cut the enemy, but he didn't have the strength to decapitate. "Your death will have to wait." He kicked the Kurjan beneath the jaw and bones snapped.

Faith screamed and looked frantically around.

Ronan turned toward the other soldier. He was speaking into his wrist. But he didn't move. Somehow, he must be calling for backup. Ronan snarled, wanting nothing more than to decapitate both monsters. But he had to get Faith out of there and center himself.

She stared in shock at the Kurjan. "You killed him."

"No." Ronan reached her and wrapped an arm around her waist, lifting her and running toward the exit. She started to struggle. An open doorway to his right caught his attention, and he moved inside a closet with what appeared to be clothing on the shelves. Blue and flimsy.

"What are you doing?" she hissed, pushing against his side.

He set her down, keeping his body between her and the door. Then he grabbed some pants and pulled them on before yanking a shirt of sorts over his head. The pants fell just beneath his knees, and the shirt pulled tight across his chest, constricting his upper arms. "What are these?" The material was unfamiliar but not uncomfortable.

"Scrubs." She tried to move past him to freedom.

He easily picked her up again and rushed for the exit, kicking open the doors with one bare foot and hurrying outside.

Fresh air hit him first, along with the darkness of night. A full moon glowed down, adding illumination to an area already lit by tall, odd candles. Different sized and colored boxes, some sleek, filled an area next to a sign that read STAFF PARKING LOT. Grass and trees were dotted throughout. One box came to life and he stiffened, growling. Lights sprang alive on its front, and it propelled itself toward them, turning at the last minute and swinging around the building.

"Teleporting devices?" he asked, awed by the thought.

"No. Cars, you dipshit," Faith muttered, kicking his side as he held her aloft. "They transport."

Ah. Fascinating. Horses had been replaced. "Which one is yours?" he asked.

"Fuck you." She kicked him again.

He sighed and shook her. "More Cyst will be arriving soon." Very soon, if they had some of these transport machines. "We have to go." He pointed Joe's weapon at her rib cage, not having a choice. "Take me to your machine, or I'll shoot you and find it myself." He'd never harm her, but apparently she didn't know that. "I don't want to kill you, Faith. But I will."

And don't miss Rebecca Zanetti's ALPHA'S PROMISE!

To hell and back . . .

Though he has vampire, demon, and Viking blood rushing through his veins, Ivar Kjeidsen's soul-crushing trip to hell broke him in ways he can barely fathom. One vow keeps the deadly immortal standing: To rescue the vampire brother who had sacrificed freedom for him. To do that, Ivar needs the help of a brilliant physicist with wary brown eyes, fierce brilliance, and skin that's way too soft.

Dr. Promise Williams understands the underpinnings of the universe but has never figured out the human beings inhabiting it. Her function is to think—and not feel—until she's touched by a vampire who's nowhere near human. The primal hunger in his eyes awakens feelings in her that defy calculation. As she shows him the way to step between worlds, he brands her with a pleasure that could last more than a lifetime . . .

Chapter One

Across the windy cemetery, beyond the rows of gravestones, a man leaned against a pine tree and watched her. Even at the distance, the deep blue of his eyes cut through the day. He stood to at least two meters, his chest broad, his legs long. His gaze was almost physical and alight with something that caught her by surprise. A rare tingling, one she'd never been able to explain to herself, much less to anybody else, morphed into an instant headache at the base of her neck.

Dr. Promise Williams shivered and broke eye contact to focus in front of her.

Meager September sunlight glinted off the coffin as it was lowered into the wet earth. The clouds had finally parted and stopped dropping rain on the mourners. She closed her umbrella and tucked it into her overlarge bag, wet grass marring her smart boots.

"It was a nice service. Earlier, I mean," Dr. Mark Brookes said at her side, wiping his thick glasses on a handkerchief. He wore a tailored black suit with a muted tie, his eyes earnest and his thinning hair wet from the earlier rain.

Promise nodded, her stomach aching. The group standing around remained silent with a couple of soft sniffs piercing the quiet. She knew all of the mourners. Six professors, a dean, and two grad students. The earlier service had been packed with students, more faculty, and even the local press. This part of the day was reserved for family.

Dr. Victory Rashad hadn't had any family. Other than the faculty, of course.

The wind picked up, brushing across Promise's face. She shivered. Who did she have? If she died tomorrow, who would attend the burial part of her service? Unwittingly, she looked toward the pine tree.

The man was gone.

Not a surprise. While he'd visited the dead, no doubt he'd just looked over at the assembled group in passing. His focus hadn't been solely on her. She shook her head and tried to dispel the dread she'd been experiencing since the police had found Victory. The woman had been missing for nearly three days before being found. Torn apart.

Who would do such a ghastly thing?

The gears of the lowering device stopped, effectively concluding the burial for the bystanders. "Well." Mark held out an arm, and she naturally slipped her glove into the crook of his elbow. "Would you like to get something to eat?" He turned and assisted her over the uneven ground to their vehicles, parked on the silent road.

"Thanks, but I'd rather go home." She'd attended an Irish wake once where the family members drank into the next day, toasting the dead with stories. A wealth of stories, and all told with love and shouts of laughter. What was it about her world that lent itself to quiet services and no humorous anecdotes? "Thank you, though."

Mark paused at her new compact car and waited for her to unlock the door. "I hadn't realized you and Victory were close."

"We weren't," Promise said quietly, opening the door. The other professor had joined the physics department at the university during summer semester, and so far, even though the school was a month into fall semester, they'd merely politely greeted each other at department meetings. That was it. Maybe a lunch or two in the cafeteria, but she didn't remember the details. "Are we, any of us, close with anybody?"

Mark scratched his chin. "I am. Two brothers, both married with kids. In fact, Mike is having a barbecue this Sunday, probably the last one before winter. I've been meaning to ask you."

"I should probably work." The idea of witnessing a happy family was too much to think about right now. What was wrong with her?

"Okay." He waited until she'd sat before leaning over the open door. "Two dates, and now I'm not sure what's going on." His intelligent brown eyes studied her, while the too-musky scent of his cologne wafted in her face. "I'm thirty-five and don't have time for games, Promise. Are we going out again or not?"

She forced a smile. "No." He was a nice man, but she'd rather work with supersymmetry or cosmological inflation than spend time with him. Of course, who wouldn't? "I think we're better situated as friends."

"Well. I do appreciate your honesty." As he straightened, his tone indicated that he did not, in fact, appreciate the truth. "I'll see you Monday." He shut her door with extra force.

Cripes. Maybe the truth had been a mistake and she should've worked harder to soften her words. Like usual.

She started the engine and pulled away from the curb, winding through the cemetery and wondering about Dr. Rashad. The police hadn't indicated any movement on the case, but Promise felt she should do something. Perhaps she'd call on Monday and request a status update.

She sped up slightly, and her doors locked. Her shoulders relaxed. It had to be a coincidence that Dr. Gary Fissure, a colleague from Great Britain, was also missing. She'd collaborated with him on a paper several years previous.

The wind picked up, and rain splattered against the windshield again. Several roads spread out in different directions. She hadn't been paying close attention when she'd driven in. How stupid of her. So she took the first left, allowing her mind to wander as she drove among the peaceful dead. She flicked on the wipers and turned down another road in the sprawling cemetery.

Suddenly, her passenger door was wrenched open and the damaged lock protested, emitting a screech-popping sound.

A man forced his way inside, rocking the car, and slammed the door. Droplets of rain wettened her leather seats.

She reacted in slow motion. How was this happening? How had he broken the door lock of her new car? Her eyes widened, and she turned her head to fully face him. That quickly, she recognized him. "You were watching me."

"I was." His voice was low and mangled, gritty and surpassing hoarse. Those blue eyes were even darker inside the vehicle.

Adrenaline flooded her, and she finally reacted, slamming on the brakes and reaching for her door. Her seat belt constricted her, but she fought it, silent in her desperate bid to escape him.

He manacled one incredibly strong hand around her arm and yanked her back into place. "Drive."

Her shoulders collided with her seat back, and she opened her mouth to scream. Her headache blasted into a migraine instantly.

He pressed a gun into her rib cage.

Her scream sputtered into a whisper. She looked frantically around, but the road ahead and behind her was empty.

"I said drive," he repeated, no infliction in his tired tone.

She swallowed, and fear finally engulfed her. The sound she made was so much of a whimper that she winced. "My purse is on the floor. Take whatever you want and get out." Her voice shook almost harder than her hands on the steering wheel.

"I have what I want. Drive." The gun and his hold on the weapon remained level. He took up more than his own seat, his arms and torso solid muscle. His face was hard and angled—cut in a way that almost looked unreal.

His words chilled through her. How was she going to free herself from him? She pressed the gas pedal again and drove along fresh graves, spotting the exit farther ahead. Her heartbeat increased its force, and her ribs ached. "What do you want from me?" She held her breath.

"Just your brain," he said, the sound raw.

She jerked, her head turning to him again. "To eat?" she gasped.

He blinked. Once and then again. "No, not to eat." His wince drew his cheeks up and his darker brows down. "Geez. To eat? Why would I eat your brain? Ick."

Her kidnapper had just said "Ick" and looked at her like she was insane. She eyed him with her peripheral vision so she could better describe him in a police report—if she survived this. At least six foot six, long dark blond hair with even darker streaks strewn throughout, handsome face. Somewhat rugged but also sharp, and with healed burn marks down his neck. His eyes were world-weary and wounded, and he'd obviously survived hell. Now she had to survive him.

Wait a minute. His words registered even deeper. Her brain? Heat spiraled through her chest. "Did you want Victory Rashad's brain too?"

"Yes."

Oh, God. He was going to kill her—just like Victory Rashad. Panic took Promise again, and she slammed her foot on the gas pedal.

"Wait," he said, grasping her arm. "I won't hurt you. I'm here to help you."

Affirmative. Yes. The guy with the gun was interested in providing assistance. Right. She ducked her head and floored the gas pedal, bumping out of the cemetery and speeding down the quiet road.

"Slow down," he hissed, his hold tightening enough to bruise.

She zipped around a corner and into traffic, driving as fast as she could.

He swore and grabbed for the key, which wasn't in the dash. She'd used the starter button. She swerved around a minivan and finally spotted a police cruiser up ahead. Slapping at him, knowing if he got her out of the car, she was dead, she took the chance of being shot in order to gain freedom.

Yelling, finally, she slammed into the rear of the police cruiser.

Everything stopped for a second and then sped up. The crash was thunderous. Her passenger bellowed and flew through the window. The airbag deployed right into her face and propelled her back into the seat.

She blinked, her ears ringing as the bag deflated with a soft hiss and a smattering of dust.

A police officer ran up and opened her door. "What in the hell?" he muttered, blood on his chin.

She coughed and shoved the airbag down. "Where is he?" she gasped, her eyesight blurry. Her assailant lay sprawled on the pavement, blood coating his face as the rain pelted down to make the red flow to the ground. The other officer leaned over him, talking into a radio at his shoulder.

Then the kidnapper jerked awake and leaped to his feet. Blood covered his face and his neck, while his left arm hung at an unnatural angle. He stood several inches above the officer. "What did you do?" he bellowed. His eyes were so dark they appeared black, and his gaze was piercing.

She screamed.

The cop tried to grab him, but he shoved the officer into the side of the car. Before the officer next to Promise could draw his gun, the kidnapper turned and ran into an alley.

The police officers quickly pursued him.

She panted, her mind buzzing, her body aching.

The police officers soon returned, both shaking their heads.

Oh, God. He was gone.

Chapter Two

Ivar Kjeidsen limped up the stairwell inside the high-rise building, blood trickling from cuts in his neck and down one arm from flying through a damn windshield. He hadn't expected the harmless-looking physics professor to defend herself so well. The healing cells he'd focused on his injuries were doing their job slowly—too slowly. The scar tissue down his neck semi-blocked the cells. Shit. He might even need a bandage, just like a human.

His boots echoed dully on the cement steps, and even though he was the only one in the entire high-rise crazy enough to climb thirty stories, the walls still pressed in too closely. But it wasn't nearly as bad as an elevator, which he'd avoid at all cost.

He'd had to walk all the way from the accident, having lost his fledgling ability to teleport the second he'd been injured. Being temporarily fragile sucked. He shoved open the door to the top floor and eyed the sheen from the white and gray tiles forming a sophisticated design down the long hallway. Beige-gray slabs of tile, thick and luxurious, made up the walls until the office opened into a center reception area surrounded by glass—one whole wall of it windows to the outside.

All glass and chrome and soothing materials.

He fucking hated this penthouse office space. It even smelled like recycled air and environmentally friendly cleanser.

Keeping his head down, he maneuvered through the hallway and past the deserted reception area to one of the many conference rooms down yet another hallway. The lights were too bright, the air too relaxed, and the height from sea level too damn far.

Banishing any hint of the pain still attacking him, he strode into the room and waited for the explosion to come.

None arrived. Instead, Ronan Kayrs looked up from a stack of maps that had been spread across the inviting and perfectly smooth light tan conference table, where he was apparently working alone at the moment. "Hello, Viking. The local news has already reported the attempted kidnapping. You had to go after her."

A familiar slash of guilt cut into Ivar. He barely kept his hand from trembling as he drew out an environmentally friendly chair to sit. "I didn't intend to take her." Sometimes his instincts still overruled his brain.

Ronan's eyes flashed a deeper aqua than usual. The vampire-demon had odd eyes, even for a hybrid. "You were on a reconnaissance mission. To watch and learn. She might be the exact wrong physicist based on the opinions expressed in some of her articles."

Ivar nodded. "I'm aware." The burn scars marring his neck went much deeper into his tissue than merely marring the skin outside, and his voice would always remain hoarse. Not as mangled as a purebred demon's, but close. Considering he was half demon, he really didn't give a shit. But right now, he couldn't let that hoarseness be gauged as weakness. "I saw an opening, and I took it."

"You failed," Ronan said simply, his eco-friendly chair squeaking as he leaned his impressive bulk back. The hybrid crossed muscled arms, looking just as deadly as the entire Kayrs vampire family was known to be, even with the recent cut to his black hair, which made him look more like a businessperson for this mission.

Ivar flushed, and his damaged skin ached. It was rare for a vampire-demon hybrid to scar, and when it happened, it hurt. Most of his burns had healed, but his neck and larynx still retained their rough texture. The inside of his throat was ribbed and uneven and annoying. Maybe hell wanted to stay with him as long as it could. "I made a mistake." One of many. When would he return to a thinking being instead of one propelled by survival instinct? He'd been trying so hard.

Ronan nodded, his mouth in a pinched line, which only accented the ones by his eyes. "She's going to be more difficult to get to now."

Ivar nodded. Taking him by surprise, a lightness caught in his chest. Nowhere near what humor had felt like years ago, but something different from pain and guilt. "She is smarter than I'd thought. Better thinking on her feet, anyway." He'd studied Dr. Promise Williams for months while he regained his sanity— somewhat—and she was obviously intelligent. But he hadn't expected her to ram her vehicle into a police cruiser. "She is in danger and needs to be locked down."

Ronan pinched the bridge of his nose. "We have got to quit kidnapping people," he muttered.

Ivar shrugged. "I don't know. It worked out well for you." Ronan had kidnapped a neurologist he'd ended up mating and adoring like a puppy that had found its place. "Where is your mate?" She was a doctor—maybe she could stem the blood Ivar still felt dripping beneath his dark T-shirt.

"Back computer room with her sister, researching that list of human physicists most likely to be targeted next," Ronan said.

"Promise Williams is next," Ivar said flatly. A couple of her academic papers had held cautions about messing with the universe, which might cause him problems. But there had been something about her. A tingling that had attacked him right before she'd tried to kill him. "And she's Enhanced." It had been the first time any of them had been close enough to her to sense her gifts, whatever they might be.

"Ah, fuck." Ronan shook his head. "I'd say the Kurjans wouldn't kill her if she's Enhanced, but now we know better." Their enemy, another immortal species, needed Enhanced human females as mates just like the vampires did.

"The Kurjans have lost their minds," Ivar muttered. The woman who'd been buried earlier that day had been Enhanced, and the Kurjans had torn her apart. Or rather, their Cyst faction, their religious soldiers, had done so. Ivar's duty began to yank him in opposite directions once again. "We have to get to her before they do."

"She might not have been on their radar until now," Ronan said.

Ivar's chest heated. "Bullshit. She's one of the best in her field, maybe *the* best, and she's next. We will get to her first." When he'd seen the crime pictures after the Kurjans had finished with Dr. Victory Rashad, even he had felt sickened. And he'd suffered through more hell worlds than he could count. They often blurred together in his nightmares. "This is as important to you as it is to me. This is our only way to save Quade. He's your blood brother."

Ronan sighed, the sound tortured. "So are you. Blood and bone, brother."

Ivar slowly nodded. Seven of them, all vampire-demon hybrids, had been bonded together in a ceremony of blood and bone that went beyond mere genetics or ancestry. "We have to free Quade, and I'm done waiting. I have a feeling this woman will get us what we need." The obsession to free Quade from a bubble world dimensions away pricked beneath his skin like live wires. His leg trembled, and he slapped a hand on his thigh to stop it. *Calm. Stay calm, damn it.* Desperation was the only emotion, the only feeling, he could truly identify these days. So he held on to it with both hands.

An elevator door in the distance dinged, and power immediately swam through the oxygen.

Ivar started to rise, and Ronan shook his head. "Logan and Garrett are finally back. Stay for their debriefing."

It was about time the two youngest members of the Seven returned from their missions. Ivar had actually missed them during the last month; they were his brothers now too. Logan had probably saved his life, and Ivar would do anything for that demon. He regained his seat. Five of his brothers, those created by the painful ritual of the Seven, had hidden him, protected him, and helped him for the three months he'd been back from hell. "You want me in a meeting? With other people?"

"I'd hardly call them people," Ronan drawled, looking up as two males entered the room. "Family doesn't count."

Ivar partially turned. "Welcome back."

Logan Kyllwood flashed a smart-ass grin. "You still batshit crazy, Viking?" He drew out a chair and lowered his muscled body into it.

"Yes," Ivar said shortly, missing his days as an actual Viking before the world had changed. Out of habit, he shared Logan's grin, even though he didn't feel what a smile was supposed to feel like. Not anymore. He'd do anything for the young warrior. He owed him. "Unlike your mate. Now that's a sane female." There was no doubt Mercy O'Malley was crazier than the rest of them put together. Most fairies were. As was Logan's mum. Maybe that was his type.

Logan snorted. "She's not crazy. Just high energy."

Fair enough.

Garrett sank into a seat with a sigh of relief. He'd been dealing with the Realm, the coalition of immortal species run by his family. His genetic family. The youngest Kayrs soldier glanced at Ronan. "Hello, Great-Uncle."

"I thought we'd finished with that nonsense." Ronan rolled his eyes. "You didn't realize I existed until three months ago, so shut up."

Garrett chuckled. "I know, but it makes you feel old and me delighted. I must be an imp."

Ivar zeroed in on the seriousness lurking in Garrett's eyes. The kid was supposed to smooth things over with the vampire king and the Realm in general. The Seven had kept their existence a secret for a thousand years, until they'd lost members and had to recruit, which had ended up outing them. Well, to nation leaders, anyway. "I take it your mission to smooth things over with the Realm wasn't roses and hugs?"

Garrett lost the grin. "Nope. The King of the Realm is a little pissed that he's still dealing with the, ah—"

"Cluster fuck," Logan said helpfully.

Garrett cleared his throat, his metallic gray eyes sizzling with intelligence. "Yes. In his words, with the mess we all have created by, ah—"

"Just existing," Logan added. "Or rather, perverting the laws of nature and the witch nation, binding our torsos into impenetrable shields, and creating a force called the Seven."

Garrett cut his best friend a look. "You are not helping."

"Not trying to help," Logan drawled.

Garrett grimaced. "I just spent the better part of a month being yelled at by several uncles, several aunts, and my mother. It was a shitstorm, and not all of us have a new mate who's happy to see us, like you do, Logan. Some of us are mateless, you know."

Logan rolled his eyes. "I know for a fact that you spent last weekend with a couple of feline shifters. Not one, but two. Female shifters are very bendy. So don't tell me you're pent up."

Garrett's lips twitched into a smile.

Logan cleared his throat. "I've been dealing with the Fae nation and trying to glean as much information about teleporting as they have learned. Unfortunately, they haven't actually studied the ability any more than we have." He leaned forward. "I've been talking to Kane Kayrs a lot, and he's getting caught up on the science behind teleporting."

Ivar glanced at Garrett. "Your uncle is willing to help us?"

Garrett nodded. "Yeah. Kane is intrigued by the whole notion, and since he's the smartest being on the entire planet, I say we tell him everything. We need to find the best human physicists and get them working with him. It's a good plan, Ivar."

Ivar nodded. "Agreed." He had to get back to that one hell world and save Quade Kayrs. His eyes met Ronan's, which all but glowed with guilt and pain. Ronan had escaped the bubble world where he'd been trapped, but Quade was still stuck in his. "We'll get him out, Ronan." It was a vow, and Ivar meant every word.

Garrett scrubbed both hands down his face. "I don't think I'm a good diplomat. It's so much easier to just hit people."

"The kid reminds me of his father." Ivar glanced at Ronan. "Though I agree. I liked it so much better when we were a secret."

Ronan nodded. "Yeah. It was easier to maneuver, but now at least we have more people working on the problems."

Garrett held up a hand. "Only the leaders of the nations know about the Seven. They're not making our existence public, by any means. At least not yet."

Ivar cocked his head. "What else did Kane say?" If the brilliant Kayrs brother was on the problem of finding Quade, then maybe they wouldn't even need to use humans.

Garrett tapped his fingers on the table. "He's been studying the cosmology of extra dimensions, cosmological inflation, baryogenesis, and dark matter. Everything every species has learned, including the humans, who actually have put a hell of a lot more time into these subjects than we immortals."

Ivar's breath caught. "Has he figured out how to get to Quade?"

"No," Garrett said shortly. "Even the Fae don't know how to find his world. The Viking here is the only one who has actually been there. When we messed with the universe to create those bubble worlds, we apparently created new rules that not even those who can teleport can follow."

Ronan leaned forward. "We did what we thought was necessary at the time."

Garrett slowly nodded. "I get that. Fourteen hundred years ago, you didn't know what we do now, and even though Logan and I are new members of the Seven, we take responsibility as if we were there and took part in the initial rituals. That might be what's pissing my uncle the king off."

Ivar could understand the king's irritation. The original Seven had created three worlds—far away from this one—with the ultimate evil, a Kurjan Cyst named Ulric, in the middle, while Ronan and Quade had manned the outside worlds as guards to keep him contained. Recently, Ronan's bubble had burst, and he was home now. It was time to bring Quade home as well. Ivar cleared his throat. "We all know that Quade's bubble will burst, or Ulric's will. So let's make it happen on our time."

Garrett lifted his chin. "Kane said that there's a chance we'll destroy *this* world if we blast open the ones created for Ulric and Quade. It's not like we understand dimensions or parallel universes or whatever the hell we created."

Ivar flattened his hands on the table, and the pace of his heart picked up. There was a piece of him, one he'd never admit to, that thought the risk of ending the world was worth it if it gave Quade a chance at survival. Yeah, that probably made him a sociopathic bastard. "Then let's get the experts in here and find out. We need to bring in Dr. Promise Williams immediately."

Ronan sighed. "You're right." He glanced at his watch and then looked back at Ivar. "She'll be here tomorrow at 9:00 A.M."

Meet the Author

New York Times and USA Today bestselling author Rebecca Zanetti has worked as an art curator, Senate aide, lawyer, college professor, and a hearing examiner—only to culminate it all in stories about Alpha males and the women who claim them. She writes dark paranormal romances and romantic suspense novels.

Growing up amid the glorious backdrops and winter wonderlands of the Pacific Northwest has given Rebecca fantastic scenery and adventures to weave into her stories. She resides in the wild north with her husband, children, and extended family who inspire her every day—or at the very least give her plenty of characters to write about.

Please visit Rebecca at: www.rebeccazanetti.com
Facebook: www.facebook.com/RebeccaZanetti.Books
Twitter: twitter.com/RebeccaZanetti

Made in the USA
Coppell, TX
17 November 2023

24386027R00090